100 OF THE BEST JOBS FOR THE JUSTICE INVOLVED

Inmates to Entrepreneurs

Malcolm Allen

D1304780

100 OF THE BEST JOBS
FOR THE JUSTICE INVOLVED

Table of Contents

Introduction

Finding a job after getting out of jail can be one of the most difficult tasks facing a felon. No one wants to hire you, but the conditions of probation require you to be employed or return to prison. Even if you have no probation conditions, you must support yourself and face the question in each application:

"Have you ever been imprisoned?"

Today, more than 80% of all employers use some form of background check, which greatly limits the work paths available to convicted felons and even those convicted of crimes.

Just because a person has been convicted of a crime does not mean that he is a bad person. Regrettably, most employers do not understand this difference. There are many reasons, many valid reasons that a person can be convicted of a crime that may even result from defending their rights or being in the wrong place at the wrong time. Many felon convictions relate to non-violent crimes, such as failure to pay taxes or refusing to testify against a friend and similar crimes, which are hardly crimes against humanity. However, these poor souls are not treated any differently from mass murder when it comes to finding a job.

This guide will assist former convicts and their families by providing a comprehensive list of large companies with a history of hiring felons and former inmates.

Attitude

The attitude you possess when searching for a job is crucial. You can quickly lose confidence by applying for three jobs, and all three ask the feared question, "Have you ever been imprisoned?" You know immediately what the result will be when you answer, and you want to leave without completing the application. The result may be different from what you think. Many companies hire convicted felons, depending on the crime, and the time elapsed. It is still right that having a conviction limits job opportunities, but there are also other avenues that many people never think of, in addition to many organizations that specialize in helping ex-convicts.

Even when things seem to be worse, try to maintain a positive attitude. This attitude will be demonstrated when you go to the interviews, and it will suffice to impress an investigator to obtain this position.

Never let the attitude of "They won't hire me anyway, so why waste my time?" When you plant this poison in your mind, you are preparing for failure. Any failure after that is the result of this attitude, which justifies strengthening the attitude. The person with this attitude never realizes that his own attitude appears in the interviews, and this negative attitude is the reason why he is not hired.

When you have a belief, you have a harder fight. Either way, finding a job is difficult, so you should expect it to be more hard with a conviction. If the average individuals go to 10 interviews, the felon may have to go through 100 interviews. Whatever number is required, it is important that you continue and work to improve with each interview. Finally, he will be rewarded.

One of the nastiest blunders you can make is to go into business and ask, "are you hiring" or "do you have jobs; I will do anything." Businesses don't want people to do anything. They want individuals who are interested in the business and who want to do a good job. They want individuals who are motivated and interested in something specific.

Now I know that no one dreams of working as a concierge or preparing food in a restaurant where they slice carrots all night, and no one studies to become a waitress. But these jobs require skills, and the person who is part of the team and wants to work in that particular company is more likely to be hired. If you are looking for a job as a waitress or waiter, say that you enjoy being with people and that you like good food and a lively atmosphere. If you know a food preparation job is open, tell the owner that you are interested in someday being a chef and try to get into food so you can learn. Telling a potential employer that you do not want to pay the rent is not an incentive for them, and it appears that you are only there to receive a salary. No smart businessman will hire you if he thinks you're just there to give him money. He wants people who work with his team and people who want to do a good job that they can be proud of at the end of the day.

CHAPTER ONE
- MINDSET

Finding a job with a crime will be difficult, so you will need to prepare for a fight. For me, the arrest was easy compared to my re-entry process when I left. Businesses that are "friends of felons" are starting to shrink, and it is becoming increasingly difficult for felons to find jobs. But you don't have to tell a former offender that he already faces discrimination on a daily basis.

You have to prepare for a fight. Enter this with a positive outlook, but understand that you will find a lot of negativity. Many HR departments and hiring managers reject your application if they find that you have checked the box "You have been sentenced." They may not say publicly that they do, but you and I know better.

Understand that it will be a fight. Sometimes you just have to smile and hang on, move until you reach the light at the end of the tunnel. Sometimes a bad job is just a stepping stone when trying to find a job with a crime.

Avoid the defeatist attitude! This is an extremely common trap for ex-offenders, and I see it all the time in the comments on Exoffenders.net. You will receive a refused job. It will absolutely happen, except for an incredible stroke of luck. You cannot , under any circumstances, convince you to give up this job search. It happened to me, I admit, and it really held me back in my first year or so after my release. It is so easy to go back to what we know, which in general, is a former delinquent ' case, it is illegal activities they landed in trouble in the first place. I think that's the major reason why the recidivism rate in this country is so high. Always endeavor to be as optimistic as you can, even when you feel incredibly overwhelmed and hopeless.

Maintain a clean appearance and good hygiene. Not only will you feel great about yourself, but you will never know when an opportunity might arise. The last thing you want when you find a job with a crime is called for an interview, and you watch as you take the form under a rock. I also explained it a bit more in a later section.

Do not worry about your past because it is your past. The fact is that when you find a job with a crime, people do it for you. You will likely have people who hold it against you when you join the company. So you really do n't need to do it either. It's your past, leave it there. It's time to move on to your future.

OPTIMISM IS KEY

In my opinion, optimism is fundamental for those who have felon convictions, but also for those who want to succeed in everything they do. If you spend all your time focusing on the negative, you won't find the positives.

In fact, positive things are likely to happen to you, but you will be so focused on the negative prospects that you will miss them.

I realize that everyone who reads this comes from a different mindset. Some of you who are reading this are probably out of prison and trying to understand the next step, while others have been unemployed for a few years and do not seem to find anything because their conviction for crime is coming to an end. through.

Whatever your situation, be aware that negative feelings and negative attitudes will get you nowhere.

Get rid of "I can't" your vocabulary and change it to "I will." As I said, it won't be easy, but you have to understand that it is possible to do what you want in a professional manner, even with a felony conviction, and having this optimistic point of view can lead to your success because you won so easily.

THINK LIKE AN EMPLOYER

When searching for a job, whether or not you have a felon record, one of the best things you can do is think like an employer. Imagine yourself sitting in front of the hiring desk during the interview process. Imagine for an instant that you have your own business and are considering hiring someone;

What would you like to see in the ideal candidate?

What kind of questions would you ask the candidate to assess whether they are appropriate or not?

Have you been in prison, what do you think about hiring your cellmate or some of the people you met while incarcerated?

I'm sure some people will come to mind, and you will think, "Yes, that would be a good employee." But there will also be people you meet and never trust or hire, and unfortunately, most people will generalize all felons in the same category.

If you start to think like an employer, you will begin to understand why they are reluctant to hire felons and what you can do to break these barriers.

Let's start by summarizing what most people will think of someone who has a recorded crime.

- Ready to break the law
- Unreliable
- Can steal things
- May be harmful to other employees
- If the felon record is disclosed, this can lead to security concerns for other employees.
- They have not worked for a long time because they are incarcerated
- Uneducated (may not be a problem if you were raised in prison)
- Maybe has a drug problem

Unfortunately, these are the kinds of things people will think of you when they realize you have a felon record. I will continue and assume that everyone who reads this guide has the best intentions in mind and that these stereotypes are not accurate.

The truth is that if you have a crime on your record, people automatically assume that you are not to be trusted. The truth hurts, but most people think so because they watch the news or see how the prisoners are broadcast on television, which is generally negative.

Later in this guide, we will see how you can combat all of these generalities, but the important thing is that you shouldn't be frustrated with the employer because he thinks that way. Obviously, the law is in effect for a reason, and regardless of what led to your arrest, you have broken the law, and it will be frowned upon.

The major point here is that you don't want to consider the thoughts that people have personally. The main reason why people think this way is that they have probably not been exposed to someone who is a retired felon who is trying to change their lives.

Think of programs like "Prison Break" and "Breaking Bad" in the two programs you are looking for the bad guy, but you would never want them to work for you.

Enter into this job search knowing that people will immediately think that way, and it will be your efforts and persistence that will show that these concerns are not justified.

MISTAKE ADMISSION IS OK

We all make mistakes. Seriously, every person I know has broken the law at one time or another.

I have many personal and professional contacts who enjoy recreational marijuana use, many contacts who have been drinking a lot (sometimes even on business trips!) And have come home, a handful of people I know who stole the property of others. Either way, people who have fought with each other and just about everyone are guilty of time theft by their employers.

If everyone I knew were brought to justice, I would bet that over 90% of them could be convicted of some sort of crime, and I am not excluded.

But you know what?

Most of them have never been captured and have no crime on their record.

On the other hand, you have a file, but that does not mean that you are unemployed.

What I'm saying is that you have to minimize your felon conviction in your head. Obviously, some felon convictions are more serious than others, but before a court, a judge sentenced him to a specified period and decided that serving a sentence would be sufficient punishment for the activity in which he was involved.

At this point, you have already taken your time and can continue your life.

If you go through all the interviews thinking that the employer can't hire you because of the crime, that's exactly what will happen.

Instead, you'd better admit the mistake and explain how you've grown since then.

If you've repeated your exact answer to someone who says, "So I saw you have a crime on your record," and it's an honest answer with information about what happened, how it was a mistake and what you did to promote yourself. and professionally since, your answer may lead to re-employment.

☐

CHAPTER TWO
- DECIDING YOUR PATH

There are five different ways that I find suitable for people who have been to prison. Remember, we are in the technology age, and one of the best ways to move forward is to adopt the tools at your disposal.

In our society, three of the most powerful tools are An Internet connection, an Internet-compatible device, and a lot of work.

If you are "ugly with computers," you have to find someone who is not ugly and helps you understand how they work, or you have to use two wonderful sites called YouTube and Google to learn. That said, here are the ways to do it:

• Work for traditional employers: take a job that is generally well below your level of intelligence and ability as a person. These are types of jobs that can almost be duplicated by machines, and you are not really appreciated as an employee because anyone can step in and do what they do every day.

- How to become a student with or without traditional education: Whether you study in a traditional college or not and pay high tuition fees or find an excellent online marketplace for acquiring the required skills, becoming a student is always a must option which can lead to a promising career once the learning curve is completed.

- Become a Freelancer: Although I think becoming a student is the first step to becoming a freelance writer, the good thing about freelance work is that you are the boss and choose the clients you work with. Your felon record doesn't matter to them as long as you finish your work and can work from anyplace, as long as you have an Internet connection and a working computer.

- Starting a website or blog: a lot of people do n't realize it, but creating a website or blog can be a fairly simple undertaking which can lead not only to self-employment, but also a scenario where you earn money. money while you literally sleep. You have probably heard of these types of businesses on the Internet, and while most are frauds, there are legitimate ways to start online businesses that make money while you sleep.

- Become a career felon: Okay, I put this option simply because some people will, unfortunately, accept it. They will think it is very difficult to do anything else, and they may also continue to commit crimes because it is the only way to know how to make a living. If it's something that comes to mind, you have to promise yourself immediately that you will get it out of your mind forever. If you can't do it, you can also get rid of this guide as it won't help.

HOW TO SECURE
A JOB WITH A FELONY

If you have been convicted of a crime, finding a job can be a very tiring and demoralizing process. In my opinion, our society makes it particularly difficult for felons and people with a felon history to get back on track. Regrettably, it is true that most employers are unwilling to hire people of felon or felon origin. Focus on most is not always the case. Here are some things to do if you are looking for a job with a crime on your record:

1. Do your research in advance

Know what is in your background check and be ready to tell employers everything they want to know if asked. Never tell a lie to your potential employer, because if he does a background check and lies to you, it won't get the job done. If you know, you will likely be asked questions about your case during the interview or hiring process, or if questions about your background have already been asked, be able to explain your situation quickly and concisely. Going into an interview without knowing what's in your background check is like driving a car blindfolded. You might be surprised at what exists and even more what may not be there.

2. Eliminate non-beginners (don't waste your time)

You need to know which companies and which types of companies will disqualify you immediately for your felon record, so don't waste time asking them. Apply for the jobs most likely to maximize the effectiveness of your job search. For example, do not waste time to apply for teaching positions or the positions of financial advisor very strict about this stuff.

There are many organizations that benefit from government tax breaks for hiring former felons. So, look for organizations like this, as you will find it much easier to find employment. More specifically, this tax incentive is granted mainly during the first year after conviction or release.

In addition, local small businesses will be more welcoming than larger ones. Large companies often have to follow strict hiring processes and procedures.

3. Don't do it alone

Whenever you are looking for a job as a former felon, don't go it alone. Look for organizations that can help you. There are many workforce development centers to help former felons find jobs for themselves. Check the center of social services in your city and see if someone can help. On the Internet, features like xamire.

4. Forget about working for someone else, start your own business

There are no limits if you have the entrepreneurial skills to start your own business, be self-employed, or be a consultant. Nothing can prevent you from starting your own business; you will face the common market threats that all entrepreneurs face on an equal footing. It is unlikely that your felon record makes a surface. Customers don't spend money on a small business background check.

5. Freelance online

Freelancing online is a good way to make money, and felon history is irrelevant. There are all kinds of jobs online, but make sure you don't get caught up in work with home scams that require prepayments. NEVER PAY A PRELIMINARY RATE FOR A JOB. The best way to get properly involved is to set up quality profiles on independent sites and bid on different jobs and tasks. You do not need to mention your felony record anywhere.

Not only is it super experienced positions in technology, but potential jobs through freelance online can also consist of personal marketing, virtual assistant, or online research. An online freelancer is a great option for those who are willing to work hard but do not have a world-class resume.

Some websites that employers, entrepreneurs, and employers of online talent are www.upwork.com, www.freelancer.com, mechanicalturk.com , and www.fiverr.com. All these companies do not charge self-employed workers in advance to find jobs and projects.

6. Resume your studies

Another smart solution would be to resume your studies. There is never a bad time to improve your education and academic skills. There are many tech jobs that only care about their skills and may care less about other limiting factors. If you can get the job done, you've been hired. Start by trying out courses at an inexpensive local community college. Take courses to keep your skills up-to-date, take a training program , or complete your GED if you still need it. It carries weight, shows that you are progressing in a positive direction, strengthens your skills throughout life, and gives you a boost of confidence.

7. Clean up your record

Depending on the type and state of crime, you may be able to remove your crime from your records legally. Do your research, find a lawyer, and talk to them about how to exclude the crime from your records. Is it costly? Most will do a free session, ask as many questions as possible! The answers, as well as research on the Internet, can help you record this yourself.

8. Get references

Getting a job offer is much easier if you have solid credentials to back it up. Select referrals who will be strong advocates for you and communicate your value to potential employers. They should be able to explain that you have worked very well on previous work or projects and that you can do this potential work. By using references, you confer the credibility of other people's characters as well as your own.

CHAPTER THREE - SOCIAL MEDIA AND SOME INTERVIEW SECRETS

Times have changed, and social media is often used by employers to find candidates and by candidates to find employers. It can be a useful asset if used correctly because social media allows you to post your work experience openly. On the other hand, be aware that social media can also ruin your chances of getting a job if you write the wrong type of message, and they are public.

People are often confused about the purpose of each social media platform and how they should use it to find a job successfully.

First, let's cover some basic rules on using social media.

Prospective employers will check their social media profiles: according to a press release created by CareerBuilder.com, just over 43% of employers used social media to select candidates in mid-2014. As companies continue to have more technological knowledge, I am confident that this number will continue to increase.

Confidentiality does not exist on social networks: whatever settings you define in your social media accounts, one thing that is always true is that these platforms will update and, when they do, can modify their privacy settings without notice. Knowing this, you need to understand that everything you post on social media can be seen by employers.

If you have pictures of yourself in the evenings, the use of recreational drugs, which poses questionable objects (like a weapon) or anything that could be considered as bad taste, I recommend you either change the privacy settings on the images you only can view or delete them altogether.

Of course, this is only a recommendation, but by eliminating these potentially dangerous photos, you are much less likely to miss image-based employment opportunities on your social networks.

Don't say anything that can cause problems: it can sometimes be tempting, in the heat of the moment, to say something you might regret later. For example, I have seen it many times when people are on Facebook on a topic like politics and verbally attacking each other's information because of their opinions on a specific candidate.

This is just one example, and there are many others, but the point you need to understand is that once you say something on social media, it may never go away. Sure, there is the delete function, and you can delete the content you have written, but it is possible that an individual will take a screenshot of what you said and use it against you.

Regrettably, this is something that happens quite often, and you don't want to be the one who wrote an angry message that ends up being posted on public forums and goes viral. My advice is to be clear, to be socially educated, and to limit their use. If you have something you would like to tell someone about, call it or meet it in person instead of writing everything down so the world can see it.

Positive content can change perceptions: the general consensus on social media is that it's the "real" you. In other words, what you say on your Facebook or Twitter profile shows how   You are in your daily life. A great way to take advantage of social media is to post positive content and always write things that are nice to others, as well as share interesting articles related to your industry. It is possible that if an employer is about to hire you because of a felony conviction when reviewing their social media profiles, they will see many positive things and be ready to risk it.

Social media can be an incredible place to meet new contacts: Social media can be an incredible place to make contacts in a specific industry or job in which you want to work. Facebook has groups, LinkedIn has LinkedIn groups, Twitter has several live performances. chats and Google Plus have communities.

What you need to do is fully immerse yourself in the industry or position in which you would like to work. To do this, you need to join multiple groups and actively ask and answer questions to familiarize people with you. Once you've been active in the group for a week or two, you'll probably start to see some of the same names as the people you're talking to. Do not hesitate to contact them politely and connect. Go ahead and ask questions and career advice if you have any. Who knows, they may even know of a job for which you are qualified with the employer or be able to connect you with someone else who can help you.

While we can take the next 20 pages to explain the intricacies of social media, I want to keep this guide succinct and focused on what really matters. With that, I will end this section by simply providing a basic understanding of how to use each social media platform, in my opinion.

• Twitter: This can be used for personal or professional use, but I recommend that you use it only for professional use, as it allows you to connect with other people in your area easily and to publish your personal ramblings. will probably not help you to be taken into account. works. Twitter is the most open social network, which means you can tag anyone and speak to them directly. This can be a massive advantage when looking for work, but the problem is that not everyone actively uses social media.

• LinkedIn: This is strictly a professional network, and if you plan to have a professional presence online, you must join this social network. To be successful, fill out your profile completely and use LinkedIn groups to connect with people in the desired industry. DO NOT post personal status updates here, it's essentially an online resume, and you must always behave in a way professional when you are on that network.

• Facebook: I recommend that you use this network for personal use, and if you do, make sure your profile has the appropriate privacy settings. The interesting thing about Facebook that people don't always realize is that there are large communities of people in Facebook groups, and I often use them very successfully. Remember that if your Facebook is for personal use, you should use the same profile for these groups in order to keep your posts positive and to exclude any content or image that may be considered offensive.

- Google Plus: Again, it's one of those social networks that people use both personally and professionally, but I choose to keep it strictly professional and, frankly, I don't use it that often. The good thing about Google Plus is that you can join communities and discuss industry topics in those communities themselves. It's useful for networking, but I think LinkedIn groups are more powerful simply because they are more popular.

- Pinterest: Although some people use this network to drive traffic to their sites on an individual level, I think it will be used primarily for personal use.

- Instagram: Similar to Pinterest, it is used by businesses to drive traffic to their business website, but you can use it for personal use.

- Vine: This is a social network that almost everyone uses for personal entertainment. I think it's okay, just make sure you don't give yourself an identifiable name.

- Snapchat: In my opinion, the vine and Snapchat are interchangeable in their use. As long as you own a username that is not identifiable to you, you will be okay.

- Meetup: strictly used for professional networking, Meetup is a great place to meet people locally who have the same professional interests as you. This can be a great place to network if you feel comfortable doing it yourself.

INTERVIEW SECRETS

Having an interview is usually one of the most stressful and difficult things you can do, not to mention someone who has a crime on their record.

Interviews, like any skill, require that the practice be successful. This is why it is always a good idea to apply for various jobs and even do interviews for those who do not interest you. In these cases, it is not the work, but the experience of the interviews.

Here are some useful guidelines to start the interview process. They are not in a specific order of importance but remember everyone before meeting a potential new employer.

Be Prepared: Before starting an interview, you should have already visited the company website and noted 3 to 5 facts about the company. This is particularly useful during a telephone interview because a very common question is: "What do you know about our company?" When asking this question, it's always good to rely on these 3 to 5 facts about the business while explaining everything. This indicates that you have done some researches and that you were really interested in the company before the interview. This preparation will impress your interlocutor.

Prepare the questions: whether it is a telephone interview or in person, having written or typed questions before starting the interview shows that you are ready. I usually write 5 to 7 questions before an interview. Make sure you don't ask questions that the job description or company website easily answer, as this would backfire and make you look stupid.

Good examples are:

• What does a typical day look like in this position?

• Why is the position open?

• What makes your business nicer than your competitors'?

• What do you like most about your work here?

Think like the interviewer: Before you start an interview, realize that your questions and answers must be specific to the situation that people are playing. What I mean is, don't ask the person from your first interview the same questions as the person from your second interviewer. What you need to do is think like the person who is interviewing you and answer your questions and your level in the business.

For example, if your first interview is with a senior sales associate, it makes sense to ask what a particular workday looks like, what they like to do in the business, what they think will make it successful. a salesperson, what it's like to be an employee of the company, etc.

If your second interview is a sales manager, you should ask higher-level questions like things have focused on the place where the company is going, because the department is a good place to work, your not t experience why they choose to work in the company, what are the main characteristics of the best salespeople, etc.

If you are having a third interview with someone who is a level C vice-president or senior manager, you should think of an even higher level of questioning. Questions about company management, why it is better than the competition, its history in the company, why it is hiring for the position, etc.

Remember that after answering all the questions they have, you MUST ask those questions and write them down or, better yet, type. It is normal to show that you are referring to these questions as you go through them; it will impress the interviewer that you have thought about all of this and that you have prepared yourself. Also, make sure that if you already covered a question in the conversation during the interview, say something like, "I was thinking about X, but we had already covered it. So my next question is ..." this that the question has been and has been covered, you show the interviewer what you thought during the interview and anticipated the subject.

Don't be sloppy: As proud as I am not a materialist, the reality is that a well-dressed person will make a good first impression against someone who is not well-dressed. As we said in the "Image is Everything" section, if you want to impress an interviewer, you need to be well-dressed and well-groomed.

Although I personally think that this does not at all indicate that you will be a good employee or not, it does mean that you are proud. Although it doesn't seem like much, it will influence the hiring decision.

Cover Tattoo: I understand that tattoos are a way to express yourself and give you a unique look. In fact, I personally tattoo, and many members of my family have tattoos that are visible all the time. That said, an interview is not where you want to show your ink unless you are trying to be a tattoo artist.

Many people associate tattoos with the irresponsibility and immaturity, and it is best to avoid this problem if you can. If you can't cover your tattoos, do everything you can to dress well and make a good impression.

Be well cared for: take a shower, comb your hair, shave it, dry it, everything you need to be well organized is necessary for each interview you conduct.

Again, it all depends on your appearance, and it may not seem really important, but someone who is well prepared conveys an atmosphere that cares about appearance and therefore cares about work.

Smile: Can - be one of the easiest things you can do, but many people are too nervous about moving on. It's really as simple as smiling during your interview. Interviewers want to work with nice people and are more willing to connect their team with someone who seems to have an optimistic and positive personality.

Sit upright: Your posture is another great sign of non-verbal communication that investigators will use to decide whether or not you will be suitable for the job. If you lean over your chair and whisper while you speak, the interview will end quickly, and you will not receive a job offer. Sit straight, look carefully, and smile.

Start with a little chat: right after joining an interview, one of the best things you can do to feel comfortable is to build a relationship. What I mean is, just ask, "How's your day going?" When the interviewer begins to speak, listen. Listen to what they say and react like you would a friend.

When I say that you have to react as you would with a friend, I don't mean that you have to express yourself on everything that happened in your day or complain about the number of interviews that you plan. No, what I mean is that you should respond to them with the normal flow of conversation, but certainly not discredit yourself by saying something stupid or complaining.

Don't chew gum: Let's be honest; gum is a wonderful thing and can keep your breath fresh when needed. However, gum has no place in an interview. If you start chatting and chatting while chewing gum, it is very likely that it will irritate the other person. Chewing gum is great, just do not interview him in the mouth, spit it out before entering.

Take water / coffee / soda if offered: One of the most common things that happen when you enter an interview is that the interviewee will ask you if you want some sort of drink.

Whenever this happens, I advise people to take the drink. The reason I say this is that it will help you psychologically while you are interviewing. It offers a level of comfort and allows you to feel and think about what is said as if you were in a cafe with a friend.

In addition, the interviewer also leaves the room to have a drink while you sit nervously, trying to calm yourself down. It's always a good time to take a deep breath and realize that it doesn't matter. If you refuse the drink, you will have to dive straight into the interview, and your nervousness will probably be transmitted. By taking 30 to 60 seconds longer to calm down and feel comfortable, you will feel much more comfortable at the start of the interview.

Finally, the drinks are good during the interview, because if you ask a question and don't know how to answer, just take your drink and take a sip. Not only does it make you feel confident and comfortable, but it also provides valuable 3 to 5 seconds to think about your answer before responding.

Establish a relationship before and after the interview: We have explained how you should interview the interviewer about his day at the start of the interview, but it also makes sense to try to build a relationship closer to the end of the interview. interview if you think things went well. .

Building relationships and connecting with your investigators can make the difference between whether you are hired or not. For example, perhaps during the interview, you will notice that on the wall is a photo of a professional sports team. If you also have a similar interest in this team, it makes sense to discuss what the team is doing and how terrible or terrible it is.

Asked about your felon conviction: Depending on the state you live in and the people you provide as a personal reference, you may be asked about your felon conviction during an interview. Although laws differ by state, here is a great example of how to deal with this problem.

"I'm happy you asked about it because I want to be very clear about my past. From X to XI, I had to serve a sentence in the FEDERAL PENITENTIARY OF THE STATE I MAKE. I served this sentence because, in the past, I made the wrong decisions, and I left with the wrong individuals and ended up in trouble with that.

After serving a sentence for a non-violent, non-drug crime (now is a good time to mention that your crime was not related to drugs or violence, if any, which will put employers comfortable), I changed radically and did not intend to follow this path again. I was   out of jail for (DURATION OF TIME), and I am working on getting my life back on track and on helping an employer grow his business.

When I spoke to other people, this particular error made them question my integrity, but I guarantee that I am an excellent employee and that I just want to have the chance to show you and this company, the positive work I can do. make. Also, I just want to mention that if you are willing to give me a chance and allow me to prove that I can really help your business, there is a government job opportunity tax credit available to give me a chance. "

If you are asked about a job gap: Obviously, if you have served a one-year prison sentence and there is a year gap in your work history, a potential employer will be curious as to why.

Here you have two options;

The first is that you can use honesty and explain how you made a mistake and served a penalty for something that is now in your past. Sure, you can get the details you want here, but be sure to explain to the employer what the circumstances were, how you now understand it was the wrong thing to do, what you learned of the mistake and what you did to change your life. since then.

Now is not the time to blame him and explain how someone "cheated on you" and got you caught. Even if it is true, it is better just to explain that you see the wrong people, that you are in the wrong type of environment, that you are wrong, and that you are learning and perfecting because of it.

The second answer you may have is a blatant lie. Although I do not forgive the lie, if you have already lied in your application and decided to avoid such questions in the hope that a background check will never be completed, you could easily say that you were self-employed or worked for a family business.

Again, I cannot tolerate lying to potential employers because if they think you are the best candidate and they hire you, your job can be terminated at any time if they realize you have a folder and have not revealed it. Also, it is not morally correct, and from this point on, you should always strive to make moral decisions.

Train before maintenance: just like athletes play games, you should train for maintenance. It doesn't matter if your interview is about something simple, like serving in a fast-food restaurant. The truth is that when you prepare for an interview, you will be better prepared for all of the questions presented.

Find out who you are interviewing: One thing that always impresses interviewers is when you show that you researched them. Typically, when you have an interview request, the contact person will tell you who the interviewee is. When they provide you with this information, write down their name, and use a site like

LinkedIn.com to find out who they are and what their background is.

One of the great ways to do this is to use Google and just type the following term: "[FIRST NAME] [LAST NAME]] LinkedIn [STATE] {NAME OF THE COMPANY]"

It is unlikely that anyone who interviews you will be on LinkedIn, but if they are, it is definitely a great talking point while you do an interview by phone or in - maintenance person. For example, if you let them know that you saw their LinkedIn profile and that they worked for XYZ, the interviewer would be very impressed to take the time to find out more about them.

Highlight achievements verbally: in your CV, you should always have the achievements that you have made professionally. If the achievements are in your training, your production, your sales figures, or your efficiency with a previous employer, you should always highlight the achievements that you have had in your professional career. However, it is not enough to list them on your

CV. In addition, you should also mention your accomplishments by going through the interview and reviewing them while explaining your experience.

For example, when someone asks for a general history of your work experience, it is always a good idea to explain what company you worked for, what your job was, what your responsibilities were, and what positive success you had. By expressing these achievements verbally, you will reinforce their importance and also ensure that the interviewer really knows them. You would be shocked that many interviewers do not read CVs completely; most of them just read the page.

Print 5 copies of your resume: One of the best things you can do when you enter an interview is to print at least five copies of your resume. The reason is that you never know how many people will interview you. I cannot remember how many times I participated in an interview in the hope of meeting one person; then, another is also seated at the table.

In addition to having additional copies of your resume, you must also have a copy with you so that you can follow the interviewer. It may sound silly, but it's really useful that if you're afraid of having a copy in front of you, you can reference your entire work history in sequential order. If you cannot print your CV at home, go to Kinko and print several copies.

Bring a pen, paper, and a folder: still, a time seem prepared is one of the greatest things you can do for an interview. Therefore, having a pen, paper, and a folder with your CVs neatly stacked inside will impress your interviewer.

Don't let the building fool you: as I said earlier, I think it makes more sense for those with a felon record to interview small and medium businesses. However, one thing that can be discouraging is when you arrive at the office of one of these small and medium-sized businesses, and you see that you are not in a beautiful building.

I made the mistake of thinking that an empty building means the business has no money, but I can absolutely guarantee that many small businesses don't have the most enviable offices, but you don't should not count them according to the building for which they question you.

Do not ask questions about the salary during the first interview: during your first interview with the company, whether in person or by phone, do not ask about the salary. The only exception is if you work with a recruiter, but if you work with someone from the company, you don't want to ask anything about the salary. The reason is that you must prove your value to the company during the first interview to be considered for a second interview. If, during the first interview, someone asks you what your desired salary is, there is no problem to answer.

Focus on explaining why you're good for them, not why you need the job: a common mistake for job seekers, especially if they haven't had a job in a while, is that they focus on why they really need the job. Even if you are desperately looking for a job, that does not mean that for your contact.

It may sound bad, but the truth is that the interviewer doesn't really care if you need the job, he cares about what you bring to the business. If you focus on telling the company why this is good for them and how much value you bring, then this is a much better conversation.

Mention specific relevant situations: When reviewing your work history, feel free to present examples of things you did with previous employers that could be considered a skill for this new employer.

For example, if you made sales in your last job and this new job is looking for a salesperson, you should certainly be talking about a difficult client you worked with or a large account that you closed and the way you did it. By linking previous work experiences to the current employer, this will prove their value.

Do not be combative when challenged: you may not like it, but there will be people who will interview you on bad days. In addition, there should be people interviewing you who may be rude. In either case, instead of getting angry and   Annoyed by the comments they can make during the interview, do your best to answer questions honestly and smile. Unfortunately, we never know who we're going to interview, and some people just don't know how to talk to other people.

Have a firm handshake and eye contact: regardless of your weight, height, or whether you are a man or a woman, you must have a firm handshake with the investigators and establish eye contact. A handshake is usually the first impression people have and the last memory they have of you before going out. If you have a firm handshake with eye contact, it shows that you are confident and comfortable. I wouldn't say that you could potentially waste an entire job opportunity based on handshake and eye contact, but it certainly doesn't hurt.

☐

CHAPTER FOUR
– BECOME A STUDENT WITH OR WITHOUT TRADITIONAL SCHOOLING

When I talk about becoming a student, a lot of people automatically assume that I'm talking about going to college. Usually, the answer is, "But with a crime, I can't go to college anyway!"

First of all, this statement is not correct. It is possible to go to college with a crime, but there are many factors that determine whether or not you are accepted for financial assistance.

Second, this is not the type of student I am talking about.

You see, many people think that the only way to succeed professionally is to get a university degree.

Although I personally think that a diploma will help you and that it is an excellent "insurance policy" for the job, it is NOT a requirement.

However, what is required is that you are trained in the skills required to do the job and develop a good job record. I know, I know, now you may not have the skills or a good track record, but it's okay.

The idea of becoming a student is not to sit in class for 3 to 4 hours at a time and listen to theoretical lessons. Instead, I advocate using the various online platforms available to learn skills, then find freelance work to test how good you really are.

If this seems overwhelming or impossible, keep reading.

It's really not impossible, and as technology has become such an important part of our lives, there are a ton of resources accessible to get you around right away. Indeed, depending on your level of motivation, it is possible that you will be trained and freelance for other companies in the next 30 days.

But this part of the guide does not include concern freelancing; it is the next section. For now, let's keep talking about how you can develop the skills you need to have confidence in your skills while working for others.

NEED SKILLS TO SUCCEED

To become a consultant or freelancer for any business, you will need to have a specific skill set to be successful. While I firmly believe that the best type of skill you learn is at work, having a hard time finding a job makes it impossible. But that's good; there are many resources available online that can provide the skills to be successful.

First, there is traditional schooling, and while this feature is good for theory-based learning, it does not always apply very well in a real work environment. What I mean is that in many classes, you will sit in a room with 20 to 500 other students and hear from a specialist in a specific field who has studied a subject for a long time, teaching what works and what does not work and how things have changed in the industry. This is how traditional education generally works, and while this is beneficial to some extent, it is not very useful if you wish to acquire professional skills.

Instead, think about what would happen if you went to a business school. In these types of schools, it's a lot more hands-on learning, and instead of focusing on theories, you focus on applying the skills you learn. However, the problem with trade schools is that some of them may not accept you because of their felon history, or you may not be eligible for financial assistance.

So, what can you do?

If you've exhausted your options or they just don't seem right, I recommend using a platform like Lynda.com. This business was recently acquired by LinkedIn.com and, in my opinion, offers the highest quality courses. The platform offers more than 3,500 courses, focused on subjects that will provide you with highly sought-after professional skills.

The greatest help you can render for yourself is to start a 10-day free trial and jump right into a course that you would really like to learn. If you want my recommendation, I suggest you go to the marketing classes and see what is available there.

Obviously, this is my preference because I am a marketing specialist, but they also have courses focusing on animation, audio, and music, general business, CAD, design, web development, l, computers, photography, and video.

The reason why this is a good idea is that our society as a whole is on the path of becoming more and more dependent on technology. These professional skills you can learn online will disappear not, and with a free trial of 10 days and a cost of $ 25 a month later, this platform is an investment incredible . To be clear, have an association here will give you unlimited access to over 3735 courses accessible on any device, in this even on a smartphone.

TRADITIONAL SCHOOLING IS STILL AN OPTION (USUALLY)

First, if you haven't graduated from high school or GED, it's relatively easy to fix that. If you want to stay local, I recommend that you contact a local college and explain that you want to take a GED program. Local colleges often have connections to established GED programs and refer them to a source of trust.

The other option is to take online courses to receive your GED. Online education is no longer a fashion and has become popular over the past 10 years. The main thing to follow on this route is that you need to make sure that the school you choose to attend online has the proper accreditation.

If you are wondering, accreditation essentially means that a third-party organization verifies the schools' GED program to ensure that it meets the Ministry of Education standards. If the program has only been accredited, you can also throw your money away. Even if you follow the program and get your "GED," it will be nothing more than an unnecessary piece of paper, as the school has not been recognized as an approved resource for those seeking education.

Now let's go to college.

There are two very common thoughts that offenders have when thinking of going back to college.

- I can't afford to go to college because it's too expensive
- I can't be accepted to college with a crime

What if I tell you that these two thoughts are incorrect?

First, let's discuss the idea that the university is very expensive.

While this is true (believe me, I could barely go to university for the same reason), are you aware that there are several cases where you can get financial aid to pay for your education? Part of this money is completely free, while part of the money is in the form of student loans, which you can pay off later at a low-interest rate.

One of the most common misconceptions about those who have committed a crime is that they are not entitled to financial assistance, and this is not entirely true. Although there are certain limits to receiving financial assistance, in many cases, it is still possible even if you have a crime on your record.

Based on our multipoint survey and the federal student aid website, here is the best explanation I can provide to explain whether or not you can get financial aid to pay for your college education.

The federal student assistance program was created specifically to help prospective students attend college, even with limited finances, by donating free money. This free money shows in the form of "Pell Grants," as well as unsubsidized and subsidized federal student loans that must begin to be repaid six months after graduation, although you can extend this date if you are having financial difficulties.

There are three very specific situations that can make a person ineligible for federal student aid:

- Not an American citizen

- Default on a previous student loan

- Convicted of a drug-related crime while enrolled as a student and receiving federal student aid.

The key to number 3 is "while you are enrolled as a student" and "while you are receiving federal money for student assistance."

You are still qualified to receive federal student aid if:

- Your felon conviction is not related to drugs or

- Your drug conviction occurred while you were NOT a student, or

- Your conviction for a crime occurred while you were a student, but during a period when you did not use Title IV money (if you paid for your lessons using money or private grants).

The federal student assistance program is very specific, and all situations are studied carefully. For instance, if you were charged with a drug-related crime while you were in college but were not actually convicted until after you left college, you would still be qualified. In fact, even individuals who have been convicted of a drug-related crime that has undergone approved treatment can be re-enrolled and accepted for federal student aid.

The reality of the university is that it's expensive, but that shouldn't stop you. The federal student assistance program is designed specifically to help those who need it, and you may well be eligible.

In addition to the federal government, you may also receive assistance from:

- The state in which you live
- The college you attend
- Private and non-profit organizations

GETTING ACCEPTED TO COLLEGE WITH A FELONY

Contrary to popular belief, having a crime does not necessarily compromise college acceptance. Many colleges go beyond crime and are willing to accept it, but unfortunately, there is no clear answer for all colleges.

The two things you need to understand when applying to college for a crime are:

- As mentioned above, your financial assistance may be limited.
- You must be very careful about the classes / concentration you focus on.

We've already talked about financial aid, so let's focus now on why you should be careful about the concentration you choose and the classes you take.

Obviously, when you go to school, you take classes to graduate for a specific job or career. For example, many people will start a nursing business because it is a great career, lots of work available, and a living wage.

However, as a felon, it would be a terrible concentration for you to work. Why?

Because nursing needs a state license, and if the state does not allow you to have a license due to a crime, you will lose years of your life and a lot of money in the process. It is also essential to realize that the colleges are there to educate you and are ready to give you a chance to improve, but you should definitely talk to an admissions consultant about your crime and be as honest as possible. Ask them about their career options and work with them to develop a plan for their future.

Once the admissions consultant has explained what you can expect, it's not difficult to get a second view from someone else to confirm everything you've been told. It may sound like an exaggeration, but it is a much better idea to do so than to follow a full educational program and find that you can never be employed anyway.

Now, if you have a drug conviction, a sex offense, or a violent crime, the college may not accept you. Although some reports show that felon records are not necessarily equivalent to problem students on campus, there is little regulation regarding the acceptance of colleges because of a crime on their records, so it is up to schools to decide.

If you think that being a student on campus is not possible, that's good! There are many distance learning programs that are of high quality and even allow you to take classes outside your home or a local library.

It may seem strange to go to school on the "computer," but be aware that it has become common for job seekers to be hired with a college degree in distance education. In fact, I have a bachelor's degree and an online program myself, and it never stopped me professionally.

NON-TRADITIONAL SCHOOLING WORKS TOO

If you don't sit in class every day or use a computer to type discussion forums and write articles, there are other alternatives to traditional teaching. We have arrived at a time in our society where technology is everywhere, and it is easier than ever to stay at home and work on the computer to live.

In my opinion, I think everyone should take advantage of this and find a way to get the training they need to succeed professionally. Most of you are probably wondering how it works, but it's much easier than you might think.

The best thing regarding the internet is that it allows people specializing in a specific subject to easily create courses that can be consumed by the general public. While this information is extremely expensive and sometimes requires an individual to travel to a specific location to attend a workshop, this is no longer the case, and now courses can be taught virtually, it has really changed the game.

In my opinion, there is no better skill than that relevant to the technology industry.

For example, what do you think are the top three companies in the United States today?

Chances are at least one of these companies, and maybe two or even three of these companies are technology-related. Whether it's Apple that creates technology products, Google, which operates the world's largest search engine, or Facebook, which is the world's largest social media platform, all of these companies are technology-focused.

Although I cannot promise that you will be hired in any of these companies, I can promise you that if you decide to focus on courses in a specific technological skill, such as web design or Internet marketing, there will be a lot of work for you in the way.

I have already recommended Lynda.com as a learning platform, but I realize that they have a strong emphasis on technology, and that is why I think they are the best place to learn your skills. I have used them several times for training, and each time, I am never disappointed with the result.

CHAPTER FIVE
- ENTREPRENEURSHIP

Getting decent jobs for felons has become an increasingly difficult task for almost everyone today. However, it has never been easy for people with a felony record. In fact, having a felon record will halve your chances of reaching the next stage of the interview. Unfortunately, this affects a large part of our society.

In fact, the numbers are incredible. You don't even have to go to the felon record to get 7-digit numbers. The US Bureau of Justice analysis reported that 1 in 110 adults in the United States is in prison. And although it may appear like a very large number, keep in mind that 0.91% of American adults are just over 2.2 million people! (1)

And that doesn't even count people currently on probation or parole. This would represent 4,751,400 additional people (at least in 2013). If you combine these numbers, you will reach 6,899,000 adults currently under correctional supervision. This means that one in 35 adults is currently in the system.

If you add a felon record to this calculation, the result may shock you. According to Andrew Cuomo, governor of New York since 2011, 1 in 3 adults has a felon record (2) . And this is where the problems start.

In New York State, more than half of those on probation were unable to find employment for themselves. And, according to research by the Center for Economic and Policy Research, nearly 2 million people in the United States are struggling to find jobs because of their records.

However, if you are one of those trying to find a job for felons, don't despair. There are career paths that you can follow to make sure there is room for you in the workshop, after all. So what jobs can you search for if you want to fight for your second chance? Read on to find out.

TOP 100
BRANDS WHO HIRE FELONS

The following list of companies that can accept felons should be used as a starting point for felons and former inmates looking for work after their release from prison. The companies listed below are also known to offer jobs to felons and, apparently, do not guarantee that you will get a job there. You will need to check the hiring site, do the research, and follow the application process normally.

AAMCO

AAMCO is the world leader in the repair and maintenance of gearboxes with centers in the United States and Canada. They are not only experts on their transmission, but they can diagnose and treat any problems you may have. AAMCO offers complete multi-point inspection, warranties, and repairs to your brakes, engine, air conditioning, and more.

AAMCO is an American repair and distribution franchise founded by Anthony A. Martino (who took the first letter of each name to arrive at the names AAMCO then MAACO) and Robert Morgan in 1957 in Philadelphia. Martino ended his AAMCO affiliation to head the MAACO auto parts franchise, but Morgan continued with his son, Keith Morgan, taking over from him as CEO. In 2006, the organization was acquired by American Capital.

ACE HARDWARE

Ace Hardware Corporation is the second-largest dealer-owned cooperative in the United States. The cooperative collects purchases and promotions for its 5,100 local hardware, center , and wood stores located in the fifty United States and in 65 countries and foreign territories. Ace's focus on service and modern retail techniques has helped locally owned and operated stores to face intense competition from home improvement powers such as Home Depot and Builders Square. The cooperative manufactures its own paint line and also supplies other products under the Ace brand.

ALLIED VAN LINES

Allied Van Lines is an American moving organization founded in 1928 as a non-profit cooperative owned by its member representatives on the east coast of the United States to help organize the return of goods and minimize dead positions (i.e., driving trucks without loading) on them). In 1968 it was reorganized into a public joint-stock company. In 1999, it merged with its largest competitor, North American Van Lines, and the combined entity became the holding company Allied Worldwide. In 2002, Allied Worldwide changed its name to be SIRVA, Inc., which went public the following year as the largest relocation and pickup logistics company.

Setting the industry standard means having the right team in place. They believe that their employees are what distinguish them from the markets in which they operate and will be the engine of their competitive advantage. They are constantly on the lookout for high energy and highly motivated talent who have a passion for winning and are excited to be part of a rapidly evolving business service company.

ALDI US

Aldi is one of the favorite supermarket chains in the United States, offering the best value for cash. Every day, they sell high-quality merchandise at the lowest price to an ever-growing customer base. Over 45 million satisfied customers regularly leave their mark on Aldi stores every month.

The company offers an easy, no-frills shopping experience to all of its customers. Delivering products at the lowest price is your strength. They did this by cutting back on non-essential features to keep the price down.

Aldi South has a good stake in the American supermarket segment. Aldi operates in 11 nations, has 5,903 stores, and 85 centers of distribution, with about 12 600 employees on its payroll. The company generated sales of 51.8 billion euros.

Aldi opened its first IOWA store in 1976. In recent decades, they have grown outrageously and now have 1,900 stores in 36 states. They employ over 1,000 people. Presently, they are among the fastest-growing retailers in the country and, by 2022, expect to reach their target of 2,500 stores.

They meticulously select most of the items in their racks to ensure high quality and the best prices. The company does not compromise these two factors because it is the core business.

Full decentralization of its operations is essential to shaping Aldi's positive growth. The product lines are designed to meet the needs of customers across the country and adhere closely to regional demands.

Aldi is a global retail supermarket chain. This opens the door to huge job opportunities. As an Aldi employee, you are in the position of being paid more than your colleagues in other similar stores. In addition, when you refer an efficient worker to apply for ALDI, you receive paid incentives.

The business nature requires greater interaction between customers and employees. This implies that staff is only selected after careful consideration of their reliability, honesty, and general approach to the customer. That said, Aldi is very precise about who they hire and where.

Aldi does not have an employment policy as to whether or not to hire a felon. The important consideration is that they comply with state and federal laws when recruiting new employees. The policy also states that a conviction will not prevent a candidate from being considered for employment with Aldi. If the crime had been committed for a long time, they would consider the job seeker. However, the process involves certain procedures to which they strictly adhere.

AMERICAN GREETINGS

American Greetings Corporation, LLC, is the world's largest greeting card company. Based in Brooklyn, Ohio, a suburb of Cleveland, the company sells paper cards, electronic cards, party supplies (such as wrapping paper and decorations), and expressive electronic content (for example, ringtones and pictures for cellphones). In addition, the company has the brands Carlton Cards, Tender Thoughts, Just For You, and Gibson.

They provide a work environment that inspires creativity and provides challenging and rewarding work in a variety of functional areas that require new ideas from many different angles. They are looking for diverse and highly motivated talents to help them change the needle in the social expression industry. They regularly recruit for a variety of positions in the business, including marketing, illustration, design, art direction, writing and editing, interactive and information technology, business analysis, sales and finance, and many others.

AMAZON

Amazon, a multinational giant, created by Jeff Bezos on July 5, 1994, is a name known for its size and professional practices in delivering products to customers around the world. Based in Seattle, Washington, Amazon today is not only a book market but also a variety of items ranging from toys, electronics, software, video games, clothing, furniture, food, and jewelry. Amazon is currently ranked as the largest e-commerce market in the world. It is a very large private employer in the United States and offers wonderful opportunities for the right people.

Amazon has many entry-level jobs spread across thousands of sites in the United States and around the world. The most common entry-level jobs are in warehouses as a storekeeper. It is a job in the Amazon warehouse and involves the selection, packaging, and shipping of customer orders. Another entry-level job is as a seasonal delivery associate, and that job requires you to deliver a package to your home and other locations.

Amazon is a technology giant that operates in many areas, so its human resource needs are very high. You can see it at the current number of 115,120 employees in the United States. As a former felon, having a job at Amazon is a big benefit not only to make changes in your life but also to grow in the future.

Amazon believes in a customer-centric business. To this end, its teams around the world are strong and determined to make life easier for customers. They believe in employing the best talent to create the leading exceptional. The company has no specific policy on hiring former felons. They have different policies on a case-by-case basis. However, unofficial sources have revealed that they employ former felons.

APPLE INC

Apple Inc. is an American international company based in Cupertino, California, which designs, develops, and sells consumer electronics, software, online services, and personal computers. Its best-known hardware products are the range of Mac computers, the iPod multimedia player, the iPhone smartphone and the iPad tablet PC.

Apple is an equal opportunity employer, committed to inclusion and diversity. They take positive measures to guarantee equal opportunities for all candidates, regardless of race, color, religion, sex, sexual orientation, veteran status, gender identity, national origin, disability, or other characteristics protected by law.

Apple will not discriminate or respond to applicants who request, disclose, or discuss their compensation or that of other applicants.

Apple will consider all qualified applicants with a felon record for employment in a manner consistent with applicable law.

Apple partakes in the E-Verify program in some locations, as required by law.

Apple is committed to working and provide reasonable accommodations to applicants with mental and physical disabilities. Apple is a drug-free workplace.

ARAMARK

Aramark Corporation, known as Aramark, is an American foodservice, facilities and clothing supplier that supplies businesses, educational institutions, sports facilities, federal and state prisons, and health establishments. Its headquarters are located at the Aramark Tower in Center City, Philadelphia, Pennsylvania.

Aramark Services, Inc. provides installation services. The company offers uniforms, food , and other related services. Aramark Services serves the education, healthcare, sports, entertainment, business, and government sectors worldwide.

Every day, they attract the most promising people to work in a wide range of industries and offer them the opportunities and benefits that underpin their careers and lifestyles.

Start by joining their talent communities and gain an advantage by being the first to know about new jobs that match your backplane and get exclusive invites to events of hiring.

AT & T

AT&T Inc. is an American international telecommunications company headquartered in Whitacre Tower, in downtown Dallas, Texas. AT&T is the second-largest mobile service provider and the largest provider of landlines in the United States and provides broadband pay television services. AT&T is the third-largest corporation in Texas (the largest non-oil company, behind ConocoPhillips and ExxonMobil only, and also the largest company in Dallas).

They expect employees to be honest, reliable, and operate with integrity. Discrimination and unlawful harassment (including sexual harassment) in the workplace are not tolerated. They encourage success based on our individual merits and abilities, regardless of race, color , religion, national origin, sex, sexual orientation, gender identity, gender age, disability, marital status, citizenship status, military status, veteran status. protected or employment status. They support and comply with laws that prohibit discrimination wherever we operate. AT&T takes full consideration of all qualified applicants, including those with a felony record.

AUTOZONE

AutoZone, Inc. is one of America's leading retailers of auto parts and accessories. The organization was founded by Pitt Hyde on July 4, 1979, and became known as Auto Shack. The corporation is headquartered in Memphis, Tennessee, United States, and is present at 6,003 locations in the United States, Puerto Rico, the United States Virgin Islands, Brazil, Mexico, and China. In 1987, Auto Shack officially became AutoZone. In 1989 the company started to computerize its store management system and also started to market a new range of batteries for Sub Zero, Desert, and long life, with the Duralast seal.

AutoZone is among the leading auto parts and accessories retailers in the aftermarket. With their presence in more than 6,000 sites, they have a huge need for qualified and experienced personnel. Although they have no clear policy on hiring felons, they have employed felons in the past and continue to do so right now. For the right person with the right qualifications and experience, AutoZone is the ideal employer.

AutoZone is in a business that requires regular customer-employee interaction. Therefore, the team selected must be reliable and honest and should not cause any problems. This implies that the team should only be selected after careful consideration. They assess the character of the person and the general approach of the client. That said, the company is very specific about the people it employs and where.

AutoZone has no written policy on the employment of felons. However, being an employer guaranteeing equal opportunities, AutoZone follows the EEOC (Equal Employment Opportunities Commission) guidelines for the employment of people with a felony record.

BLACK AND DECKER

Black & Decker Corporation is an American manufacturer of power tools and accessories, hardware and home accessories, and technology-based fastening systems. On March 12, 2010, Black & Decker merged with Stanley Works to become Stanley Black & Decker. It remains a subsidiary hand full of this company but has its own headquarters in Towson, Maryland, a suburb of Baltimore.

BUFFALO WILD WINGS

Buffalo Wild Wings Grill & Bar is an American casual dining and sports bar franchise in the United States, Mexico, and Canada, known for its Buffalo wings and sauces. The restaurant's current slogan is "Wings. Some beer. Sports. "

Buffalo Wild Wings has an atmosphere that creates stories that are worth telling your guests and staff. Yes, it literally works in a sports bar and all the energy that goes with it. But Buffalo Wild Wings is also a place to start the next phase of your career. If you grow up on their system here at Buffalo Wild Wings or if your game plan finds you elsewhere, they want you to have a lifetime experience here. They are a rising brand and need great people when they write the next chapter in their story. If it's you, pull a stool.

BRAUM'S INC

The Braum Ice Cream and Dairy Stores (pronounced br- ah- ms) is a family-owned and operated chain of fast-food restaurants and supermarkets headquartered in Oklahoma City, Oklahoma. To maintain the freshness of its products, the company does not open stores within 483 km of Tuttle Farm, Oklahoma. As of November 2013, 280 stores were in operation, including 128 in Oklahoma, 99 in Texas, 27 in Kansas, 13 in Arkansas, and 13 in Missouri.

BIG LOTS

Big Lots offers everything from consumables, household items to toys, and seasonal items. Big Lots is a community retailer dedicated to friendly service, reliable values , and solutions that are affordable in all seasons and categories - furniture, food, decorations, and more. Starting as a settlement store, Big Lots is now retail at a reduced price, with the primary goal of helping people save money on all types of products.

Big Lots currently employs approximately 23,000 people at more than 1,400 locations. True to its principle of hiring people who will flourish, the company offers many advantages to its employees. Health care, retirement planning, the company paid life insurance, investment opportunities in savings plans, short and long term disability protection, and other additional benefits such as premium plans , vacation plans, the company paid vacations, educational assistance, and merchandise discounts. These are some of the benefits they offer their employees.

Big Lots is not officially registered with the Ban the Box movement, which encourages the removal of the box by requesting details of the applicant's felon history on the application form. However, in principle, they are committed to providing jobs for everyone, including those with felon histories, and this is explained below.

The company is committed to the principle of equal employment opportunities for all its employees and also offers them a workplace free from discrimination and harassment. All employment decisions are based on business needs, job requirements, and individual qualifications. Doing this, they do not discriminate against people.

Above all, they are ready to employ qualified people with a felon record. The only consideration is that it will be based on the laws, regulations, and ordinances applicable in this particular area. As a felon, this company decision will benefit you because it leaves the door open for you to look for a job at Big Lots, despite your felony history. With the right qualifications and experience, you have a good chance of being employed at Big Lots.

The company also does not officially support the Fair Chance Business Pledge, which hopes to give all job seekers an equal chance and does not let their experience play a role in the recruitment process. Although they have not kept that promise, Big Lots offers good luck to anyone applying for a job.

CARL'S JR

Carl's Jr. is the perfect opportunity to find important jobs in the fast-food industry. Workers can find jobs fast food that the employees part - and full-time - time in the functions of management and entry.

The fast-food establishment maintains full operations in the western and southwestern United States, as well as in several countries throughout much of the world, including Russia, China, Brazil, and Puerto Rico. Applicants can find work with room for professional growth in fast-paced, fun environments in over 1,300 locations.

Job seekers aged 16 and over seeking catering experience must fill out an application form immediately. Carl's Jr. jobs offer a competitive base salary, generous salary options, paid training opportunities, flexible work hours, and a stimulating work environment with potential for career advancement. Workers must have exceptional customer service skills as the fast-food chain entertains thousands of customers daily. The ability to cope with high-stress situations and maintain an effective work ethic is also required for the job.

CATERPILLAR INC

Caterpillar Inc. is an American company that designs, manufactures, markets, and sells machines and motors and sells products and financial insurance to its customers through a global network of dealers. Caterpillar is a world frontrunner in the manufacturing of mining and construction equipment, diesel and natural gas engines, diesel-electric locomotives, and industrial gas turbines.

At Caterpillar, you can build your career the way you want. They are looking to hire a variety of skills, experience levels, and qualifications. Sign up - if they and develop professionally, want to work with them for a while or during your career. Your employees have the opportunity to create a varied CV by following different careers at Caterpillar - by moving between its many business units, functions, or sites.

Ready to put your passion into practice? Explore Caterpillar workspaces and sign up today.

CDW

CDW Corporation, headquartered in Vernon Hills, Illinois, is a provider of technology, business, government, and education products and services. CDW was originally incorporated as "MPK Computing" by its founding member Michael Krasny, who currently ranks on the list of Americans the richest Fortune. It later became Computer Discount Warehouse, then simply CDW.

CDW is an equal chance / affirmative action employer engaged in a diverse and inclusive workplace. All eligible applicants will be considered for employment regardless of race, color, religion, sex, national origin, protected veteran status, disability status, sexual orientation, gender identity, or any other basis prohibited by law.

CHILI'S

Chili's Grill & Bar is an international casual restaurant chain offering Tex-Mex style cuisine. The organization was founded by Larry Levine in Texas in 1975 and is currently operated and owned by Brinker International. Chili's is the leading casual dining company in the world and has received numerous awards over the years for its excellent performance.

CINTAS

Cintas Corporation is an American organization that provides specialized services to companies of all types, mainly in North America. Based in Cincinnati, Ohio, Cintas designs, manufactures and implements uniform corporate identity programs and provides entrance mats, bathroom cleaning, and supplies, tile cleaning, and carpets, promotional products, first aid, safety, protection products, and services. fire for business.

COMMUNITY EDUCATION CENTERS

Community Education Centers, Inc. (CEC) is a leading provider of re-entry treatment and education services for adult prison populations across the United

States. CEC is firmly committed to a partnership with government agencies to provide intensive re - the input processing programs and the education that put the emphasis on change dependency and felon behavior, the preparation of offenders for re-entry and ultimately reduce recidivism.

COCA-COLA

Coca Cola is an American multinational company that manufactures and markets soft drinks and syrups. The company's flagship product, Coca Cola, is a world-class non-alcoholic drink and one of the best-selling drinks on the market. The Coca Cola formula was invented in 1886 by pharmacist John Smith Pemberton in Atlanta, Georgia. Pemberton accountant Frank M Robinson named the product the historic name Coca Cola. The word Coca Cola is taken from the 2 ingredients, the coca leaves and the cola nuts from which the drink is made.

Coca Cola is a global beverage manufacturer with a presence in 200 countries. This offers job opportunities worldwide and particularly in the United States. Your hiring policy does not specifically mention the hiring of former felons. They have an internal policy regarding the crime committed, and this is strictly confidential. Research of its hiring records revealed that the company had hired felons in the past. Of course, certain conditions apply, and they will be covered in the following sections of this book.

Coca Cola complies with the laws of the state in which you are seeking employment. This is an important consideration when recruiting new employees. This unwritten policy does not disqualify a felon for a job. However, the selection process involves certain procedures that are strictly followed.

COSTCO

Costco Wholesale Corporation is an American multinational. It is also known as Costco. Costco operates a chain of retail stores only for members or warehouse clubs, as they are also known. Costco is the 2nd largest retailer in the world. Among the Fortune 500 companies, Costco ranks 14th based on total sales.

Costco is one of the greatest retailers in the world, present in 12 countries. With 539 warehouses in the United States, Costco has a huge recruitment demand. First of all, you must decide if you are looking for a job in the retail business. If so, Costco is an ideal choice because of its vast potential. But does Costco then hire felons? The answer is yes, referenced by different sources, but it will not be the same for each case. Generally, whether or not you are employed depends on the type of crime you commit, the length of your absence, the interviewer's point of view, and the number of job seekers at the time.

However, from Costco, they did not directly disclose their policy for hiring ex-felons. They did not provide information on hiring policies specific to ex-offenders, and there is no information to indicate that they employed ex-offenders.

DAIRY QUEEN

Dairy Queen, often abbreviated as DQ, is a fast-food chain owned by International Dairy Queen, Inc., a subsidiary of Berkshire Hathaway. He also has Karmelkorn and Orange Julius. It serves several frozen products such as ice cream and ice cream.

Every day around the world, they offer an experience that makes their customers feel at home. From a warm smile to quick service, your team keeps customers coming back to find out more. Visit the store DQ® closer to know more about joining the family DQ. They would love to have you.

They are always searching for the right people. At the American Dairy Queen Corporation, they pride themselves on a multinational corporate culture that has successfully maintained a sense of small community, full of hardworking values, teamwork, and integrity. If you believe in working to provide magic experiences worldwide for DQ®, they want to hear from you.

DOLE FOOD COMPANY

Dole Food Company, Inc. is an American agricultural multinational based in Westlake Village, California. The company is the largest producer of fruits and vegetables in the world, with 74,300 employees working full time and seasonal, responsible for more than 300 products in 90 pa e SES.

Dole Food Company, Inc. is the world's largest producer and distributor of high-quality fresh fruit and vegetables. They also market a growing range of packaged and frozen foods and are proud to be an industry frontrunner in nutrition education and research. Present in more than 90 countries, they employ an average of 36,000 full-time employees and 23,000 full-time or temporary employees worldwide.

As a global supplier of fruit and vegetables, they are a strong supporter of equal employment opportunities. One of its missions as a global company is to treat all individuals - employees, partners, and customers - with respect.

D career opportunities ole Dole Food Company with fruits of business and vegetables Dole and divisions include marketing, manufacturing, sale, exploitation, maintenance, finance, and many others.

DOLLAR RENT A CAR

Dollar Rent a Car was launched in 1965 by Henry Caruso in Los Angeles, California. In 1990, it was acquired by Chrysler. The dollar has more than 647 locations worldwide in 53 countries, with an important presence in Europe, Latin America, and the Caribbean, including more than 358 in the United States and Canada.

If you want a career in the car rental industry, Dollar has a new job for you. They seek competitive benefits in the jobs available. Your new career awaits you, what are you waiting for?

Due to increasing federal record-keeping and reporting requirements, it is your policy not to accept unsolicited applications or CVs. Unsolicited resumes and applications are not retained and will not be taken into account when making employment decisions.

DOLLAR GENERAL

Dollar General is a family business founded in Scottsville, Kentucky in 1939. It is an American retail chain that sells a wide variety of affordable household items and snacks under its various subsidiaries. Has become one of the most lucrative retail chains in the United States, with revenues of $ 25.6 billion in es in 2018. The company currently operates 15,000 stores in the United States and employs 130,000 employees altogether.

It is compulsory to know where your employer is based on discrimination against former felons who are trying to start a new life. This way, you can judge companies in advance and apply only to those you are comfortable working with. As far as public information is concerned, Dollar General offers equal opportunities to all. This ensures that the organization has a safe and equal work environment for men and women, but it does not necessarily mean that they hire felons. Despite everything, it is still an advantage for you so far.

According to recent analyses and reports, it seems that they are open to hiring felons without a problem. Many former offenders who have worked with Dollar General in the past have testified. Many of them were hired and treated lightly by the company. They recommended that if you want to be hired, you have to be honest and open.

And Dollar General is not on the Ban the Box list or part of the Fair Chance Business Pledge; it still seems to hire people on its merits, regardless of their background. This makes Dollar General the best opportunity to try if you are accused of a felony record.

DR. PEPPER

Dr. Pepper Snapple Group Inc. (formerly known as Cadbury Schweppes Americas Beverages) is an American soft drink company based in Plano, Texas. It remains one of the leading soft drink companies in North America, manufacturing, bottling, and distributing over 50 brands of juices, soft drinks, teas, churns, water, and other premium drinks.

At Keurig Dr. Pepper, they build their rich heritage to create the beverage business of the future. Join your strong and committed team of more ' than 25,000 employees in the United States, Canada, Mexico, the Caribbean, Europe, and Asia, who deliver excellent results every day in marketing, sales, distribution, manufacturing, engineering, research and development and much more. more.

They work with great brands of coffee and exciting drinks at KDP and have fun doing it! Their forward-looking culture is the foundation of a rapidly changing environment where they dream big and love what they do. Whatever your area of expertise, KDP allows you to be part of a team proud of its brands, partnerships, innovation, and growth.

DUNLOP TIRES

Dunlop tire is a brand of tires owned by subsidiaries of Goodyear Tire and Rubber Company in North America, Europe, and Australia. In other counties of the world, the Dunlop brand belongs to other companies. In India, the brand belongs to Dunlop India Ltd., whose parent company is Ruia Group, and the rest of Asia and Africa, to Sumitomo Rubber Industries.

At Goodyear, they built their foundation on a commitment to forward-thinking innovation, and they are proud of Selves for attracting and retaining the best talent, promoting new ideas, teamwork, open communication, and opportunities. career development.

They strive to provide associates with a safe work environment and emphasize the need for continuous learning as well as a continuous experience. By offering wide opportunities for growth, they are able to maintain a long tradition of growth and promotion of talent from within.

These goals, combined with competitive compensation and benefits, they help to foster an environment in which employees can work to accomplish their full potential and contribute to the success of the company.

Join a group of committed and talented associates to help grow your business and ensure your future success. Consider starting your career at Goodyear.

DUNKIN DONUTS

Dunkin 'Donuts is a global American donut business and coffee chain based in Canton, Massachusetts. It was created in 1950 by William Rosenberg in Quincy, Massachusetts. Since its creation, the company has become one of the largest chains of coffee and bakery products in the world, with 11,000 restaurants in 33 countries of different SES. The chain has grown to include more than 1,000 items on their menu, including bagels, donuts, other baked goods, and a wide variety of hot and cold drinks.

DURACELL

Duracell is a range of products from the American brand of smart batteries and power systems, owned by Procter & Gamble. In November 2014, Warren Buffett, through his holding company Berkshire Hathaway, acquired the brand for $ 4.7 billion.

Join the Duracell staff and lead an exciting reinvention of the distribution network of one of the most emblematic brands in the world. Duracell is the world leader in batteries, with more than $ 2.4 billion in annual sales. In 2016, Duracell joined Berkshire Hathaway, a multinational conglomerate of American holding companies. Berkshire is led by Warren E. Buffett, one of the most famous investors and business leaders in the world. Berkshire employs more than 302,000 people and ranks 13th among the 500 most admired companies in the Fortune 500.

EPSON

Seiko Epson Corporation, commonly known as Epson, is a Japanese electronics company and one of the world's largest producers of computer printers and related information and imaging equipment.

Epson's team of dynamic, creative, and inventive product managers keep abreast of business trends and help keep Epson at the top of the industry curve. By analyzing market data, market trends, and researching customer information, your product managers define the direction of your needs in the North American market.

From public relations to advertising, from lead generation to trade shows, from product marketing to social and online marketing, MarComm's marketing communications team is the public face of Epson. This creative, ingenious, and inspiring team is responsible for ensuring that Epson remains the technological leader in digital solutions and innovative products.

Your sales team and your sales support team are made up of dynamic collaborators. They are the local ambassadors Epson, sharing the unique nature of the range of products from Epson with industries ranging from hospitals to hotels and major retailers in the elementary schools. If you are passionate about sales and love innovative technologies, this may be the team for you!

ERMCO, INC

Throughout its history, ERMCO has maintained its vision of being a leader in the electricity sector. Its success is achieved through customer satisfaction, the emphasis on employee satisfaction and commitment to teamwork, innovation, diversification, and professionalism.

The ERMCO, Inc. is currently seeking qualified individuals for the post office and the field.

ERMCO has been named # 1 Large Company in Central Indiana "Top Workplaces 2017" by Indianapolis Star. Employees describe the business like family and team-oriented, with strong benefits and the opportunity to grow professionally.

If you wish to have the possibility of becoming a member of the ERMCO team and of engaging in an ethical, professional, and family work environment, this may be the best time for you.

FedEx

FedEx head office is in Memphis, Tennessee. FedEx is known in the United States for its overnight shipping service. They are a reliable and premium email service provider worldwide. FedEx is a pioneer in the introduction of a system that can track packages and provide real-time updates on their sites. Today, almost all shipping companies use this system to manage their freight.

As a global delivery organization that sends and receives large packages, FedEx provides employment opportunities at every stage of the journey. As a FedEx employee, you get job security, a solid work-life balance, and other benefits.

The nature of the position you hold in the business determines whether your job may require a lot of interaction with customers. FedEx pays special attention to the people it employs for the same reason.

FedEx said the existence of a felon record is not a barrier to employment. Your felon record will be carefully and carefully examined. The time and nature of the offense will be taken into account with other necessary information before making a decision. As an equal opportunity company, FedEx Office will consider applicants with a felon record in accordance with the requirements of the Fair Chance Order. This implies that employers will not ask you questions about your felon record after a conditional job offer.

FIRESTONE COMPLETE AUTO CARE

With more than 1,600 stores and a growth of more than 50 new stores each year, Firestone Complete Auto Care is one of the largest providers of automotive and tire services in the world.

They are looking for passionate problem solvers who roll up their sleeves and are dedicated to keeping their customers' vehicles running smoothly every day, in all bays and service centers. They offer training, certifications, and the opportunity to develop your skills because they understand that investing in their employees is an investment in the future of our business.

Bridgestone Retail Operations, LLC (BSRO) operates the world's largest tire and automobile chain owned by the company, with four retail brands and 2,200 stores nationwide. Whether you're looking to specialize in retail, customer service, store management, or technical skills, BSRO is a place for great filmmakers.

If you're looking for opportunities to do what's right for vehicles and the people who drive them, Bridgestone is your way to a rewarding career. They will provide you with the training you need to take your skills to the next level.

Bridgestone's retail operations offer excellent job opportunities that combine automotive service with customer service. Your positions as a sales associate will set you on the path to a rewarding career in retail management, car maintenance, or car sales.

FUJIFILM

Fujifilm Holdings Corporation, commonly known as Fujifilm, is a Japanese multinational photography and imaging company based in Tokyo, Japan. Fujifilm's core business is the development, production, sale, and maintenance of color films, digital cameras, finishing equipment, color paper , finishing chemicals, medical imaging equipment, and graphic arts supplies, flat-screen monitors, optical devices, photocopiers, and printers.

Fujifilm strives to provide a healthy work environment that promotes individual responsibility and growth, a spirit of collaboration, and an atmosphere that encourages learning, professional development, and success.

They are looking for the most talented and qualified people for external and internal opportunities. At

Fujifilm, performance, development, and responsibility are the standards by which the company and its employees strive. And to support their employees, they offer programs that motivate, educate, and promote a healthy work-life balance that increases employee satisfaction and overall personal well-being.

Fujifilm is committed to providing a comprehensive and flexible benefits program to meet the needs of workforces and their families. This flexible approach lets employees create a program tailored to their lives. At Fujifilm, INNOVATION and PEOPLE are important.

GENERAL ELECTRIC

General Electric is an American multinational company incorporated in New York and based in Fairfield, Connecticut. The company operates in the following segments: energy [inactive 2013], technological infrastructure, capital financing, consumption, and industry.

GE is an employer guaranteeing equal opportunities. Employment choices are made regardless of race, color, religion, national or ethnic origin, gender identity or expression, age, disability, sex, sexual orientation, protected veteran status or other characteristics protected by law.

GENERAL MILLS

General Mills, Inc. is a food organization based in the suburbs of Minneapolis, Golden Valley, Minnesota. The organization markets many well-known North American brands such as Betty Crocker, Yoplait, Colombo, Totino , Pillsbury, Green Giant, Old El Paso, Hagen-Dazs , Cheerios , Trix , and Lucky Charms. Its brand portfolio consists of more than 89 other major American brands and several category leaders around the world.

General Mills is reforming the future of food. They believe that food makes us better. It nourishes our body, brings us joy, and connects us. As one of the world's fastest-growing food companies, General Mills functions in more than 100 countries and markets over 100 consumer brands, including Cheerios , Nature Valley, Betty Crocker, Yoplait, Annie's Homegrown, Old El Paso, Old El Paso, Epic Provisions, Blue Buffalo and more. Are you in love with the future of food? You have arrived at the right table. They want the best talent to help lead something big. Join them now!

GOODWILL

The laws meet the needs of all job seekers, including programs for youth, the elderly, veterans and the disabled, felon records, and other specialized needs. Last year, Goodwill helped over 9.8 million people to train for careers in sectors such as banking, healthcare, and IT, to name a few - each - and get the support services they need to succeed, such as English training, continuing education. or access to transportation and child care.

Whether it's developing skills, graduating, planning your next career, honing your job search and maintenance skills, getting your funds in order, or getting the resources you need to get ahead, your local goodwill can help!

GREYHOUND

Greyhound Lines, Inc., which was founded in 1914, is the largest provider of long-distance road transportation, serving more than 3,800 destinations in North America with a modern and green fleet. He became an American icon, providing travel safe, pleasant , and accessible e LEVELS nearly 18 million õ es passengers per year in the United States and Canada. The Greyhound dog breed is one of the most recognized brands in the world.

HANES

Hanesbrands Inc. is an American clothing organization based in Winston-Salem, North Carolina. It employs 50,000 people internationally. Hanesbrands owns several clothing brands, which are Hanes (their biggest brand), Champion (their second biggest brand), Playtex (their third-biggest brand), Bali, L'eggs, Just My Size, Hanes Hosiery, Barely There , Wonderbra. ,

Duofold , area , Beefy-T, Champion C9, Cacharel ,
Celebrity, Daisyfresh , JE Morgan, One Hanes Places,
Ribs , Rhythm , Sheer Energy, Silk Reflections, Sun, Sol
y Oro Tagless and Zorba.

HanesBrands brings people together. Their
workplaces connect diverse cultures, geographies, and
backgrounds, creating a corporate culture, unlike any
other in the world. Its more than 70,000 employees
represent more than 40 countries on six continents. Each
individual has unique perspectives and aspirations that
represent and bring out the best in everyone. Working as
a unified team, they succeed in the market, advance their
careers, and improve their global communities. They
invite you to join them.

HILTON HOTELS

Hilton Hotels & Resorts (formerly Hilton Hotels) is
an international chain of full - service hotels and resorts
and the leading brand of Hilton Worldwide. The original
business was founded by Conrad Hilton. Hilton Hotels
became the number one hotel chain from coast to coast
in the United States in 1943. In 2010, there were more

than 530 Hilton brand hotels worldwide in 78 countries on six continents. Hilton hotels are owned, managed or franchised by independent operators by Hilton Worldwide.

Hilton's policy is to employ qualified people regardless of gender, color , race, religion, national origin, sexual orientation, disability, gender identity, age, or any other protected group status as defined and subject to applicable local laws. Hilton's commitment to equal employment opportunity fosters the attraction and retention of a diverse workforce, which will increase society's competitiveness to attract members of the team, customers, business members, and owners.

HOME DEPOT

The Home Depot is a well-known and well-known chain of home decor chains widely used in the United States, Mexico, and Canada. With more than 400,000 employees, the chain offers a feeling of familiarity to its employees as well as to its customers.

There are over 2200 chain stores in North America, as well as the center's sales and support. The chain is one of the largest in the United States. Serving people who like crafts and want to develop products for the entrepreneurs known that oversee projects at the industrial level, it goes without saying that the store chain is extremely versatile in its services.

Will The Home Depot Hire You? Short and long answer, yes, they do. Support the movement to ban boxes, which implies that candidates are not asked about their past before the interviews. This allows you to prove your worth without being tried for a crime that you have committed. In addition, Home Depot has also made the Fair Chance business commitment. This promise obliges them to give everyone a fair chance to apply for this job.

That said, it is not without precaution that they do so. During your interview, you will be asked about elements related to the crime you committed. But if they find out that you are no longer the person who committed the crime, the job could be yours. You should have changed and convinced them as well. Another question that can bother you is whether they check everything you said in your interview.

IBM

The International Business Machines (IBM) Corporation is an American multinational consulting technology, based in Armonk, New York, United States. IBM manufactures and markets hardware and software, and provides infrastructure, hosting and consulting services in areas ranging from mainframe computers to nanotechnology.

At IBM, work is more than work - it's a vocation. To build. To conceive. For the code. To consult. To think with customers and sell them. Create markets. To collaborate. To invent. Not just doing something better, but to try things you never thought possible. To lead this new technological era and solve some of the most difficult problems in the world.

Deciding to kickstart your career at IBM is an investment in your future. Whether you are an undergraduate, graduate, or postgraduate student, they will help you turn your years of study into tangible achievements through a wide range of career opportunities and global development programs.

At IBM, you will find countless opportunities to build the career you've always wanted. Find out what it's like to be an IBM professional.

IN-OUT-OUT BURGER

In-N-Out Burgers, Inc. is a regional fast-food chain located in the southwest. Founded in Baldwin Park, California, in 1948 by Harry Snyder and his wife Esther Snyder, the network is currently headquartered in Irvine. The In-N-Out Burger has slowly spread from southern California to the rest of the state, as well as Arizona, Nevada, Utah, and Texas. The current owner is Lynsi Snyder, the only grandson of the Snyders .

JACK IN THE BOX

Jack in the Box, by Robert O. Peterson in San Diego, is an American fast-food restaurant founded in 1951 where it is still located today. In total, the network has 2,200 locations, primarily serving the west coast of the United States. Foods include a variety of hamburger and cheeseburger sandwiches, as well as international-themed food selections such as tacos and eggrolls. The organization also operates the Qdoba Mexican Grill chain.

JPMORGAN CHASE

JPMorgan Chase & Co. is one of the leading US multinational financial companies. He is well known for banking and investment finance. JPMorgan Chase is currently the largest bank in the United States and the sixth-largest bank in the world based on total assets - $ 2.73 trillion. It is also the world's largest market capitalization company. In addition, JPMorgan Chase is one of the oldest banks in the United States and is currently headquartered in Manhattan, New York.

It offers products that include securities trading, brokerage services, debt settlement, asset management, digital banking, currency exchange, insurance, investment banking, and hedge funds. In particular, its hedge fund is considered to be the third-largest hedge fund in the world. With such a scale, the company has hired more than 257,000 employees to date.

Will JPMorgan Chase Hire You? The answer is yes. According to Fortune, JP Morgan Chase recruited more than 20,000 American employees in 2018, and about 10% of them were former inmates. The company tries to provide employment opportunities to 10% of people with a felon record each year and also ensures that it does not threaten the functioning of the financial system. In addition, JPMorgan Chase will make significant investments of almost $ 7 million to help organizations connect and provide professional training and hands-on skills to former felons. These organizations mainly come from Detroit, Nashville, New York, Seattle, Chicago, Delaware, and Wilmington.

JPMorgan Chase also stressed that his goal now is to provide basic jobs for juvenile offenders in the past, such as DUI, low-level drug possession, and disorderly conduct. In addition, the company supports felon justice reforms to reduce fines for certain offenses and facilitate the elimination of felon records.

As one of the largest American banks, it believes in inclusion and equal opportunities for all. Therefore, you may have a chance of being hired by a reputable organization. While the financial and banking sector is difficult for former felons to find employment, it is not impossible.

KELLY MOORE PAINTS

Kelly-Moore Paints is a paint producing company founded in San Carlos, California, in 1946 by William Kelly and William Moore. It has stores in California, Washington, Oregon, Arkansas, Texas, Oklahoma, and Nevada.

Kelly-Moore offers equal opportunities to all conditions of employment. They will not discriminate against qualified candidates or employees regarding conditions of employment due to any basis protected by either local, state, or federal laws, including race, color , religion, religious dress or grooming , national origin, sex, age , marital status, veteran status, sexual orientation, physical and mental disability, medical condition, gender identity, gender expression, and genetic information.

Kelly-Moore Paint personnel is a community of people who work together to excel in their industry.

What differentiate Kelly-Moore Paint organization from the competition? These are not only your premium products but also your incredible staff! Your teams do what they need to exceed customer expectations.

You can build a solid career with them , where you will be encouraged to contribute your best every day.

KFC

KFC (the name was initially an initialism for Kentucky Fried Chicken) is a fast-food chain specializing in fried chicken and is situated in Louisville, Kentucky. It is the second-largest restaurant chain in the world (measured by sales) after McDonald's, with 18,875 points of sale in 118 countries and territories in December 2013. The company is a subsidiary of Yum! Brands, a restaurant business that also owns the Pizza Hut and Taco Bell chains.

KFC is more than a workplace; it is a place of growth! Through their training programs, training experiences, and development, they offer career growth through a variety of possibilities. Many of your managers started as team members and have evolved into restaurant management roles and more! Your training programs are rewarded, and you can even earn university credits for completing our restaurant training!

KRAFT FOOD

Created in 1903. Renovated in 2012. With a portfolio of prestigious brands and a culture of collaboration and innovation, Kraft has the soul of a start-up and the soul of a power plant. One of the largest packaged product companies in North America, Kraft has 22,500 employees in the United States and Canada and $ 18 billion in annual sales.

Kraft Heinz organization is the third-largest food and beverage organization in North America and the fifth-largest food and beverage organization in the globe, with eight brands over $ 1 billion. A world-renowned producer of delicious food, The Kraft Heinz Company, provides quality, good taste, and quality nutrition for all occasions at home, whether at home, in restaurants, or on the go.

KROGER

Bernard Kroger created Kroger in 1883 in Cincinnati, Ohio. The company has grown exponentially over the 136 years of its existence. With more than 450,000 employees, the company has a variety of stores in the United States. Some of them include hypermarkets, supermarkets, department stores, hypermarkets, jewelry stores, etc. just to name a few.

Kroger is the largest revenue supermarket chain in the United States. The company posted revenue of $ 121 billion in 2019. In addition, it was second behind Walmart and ranked 5th in the world in terms of retail.

Kroger hires felons, but only for entry-level positions. This is understandable since any higher position would require qualifications, skills, and experience. In addition, they need prior knowledge of how the business works. Entry-level jobs, however, require very little skill. This opens up opportunities for individuals with little experience. If you are an experienced and trained person in a particular field, try to apply for a higher position.

Also, there is a slight chance that you will still be excluded from the process, as the Kroger process deals on a case-by-case basis when it comes to hiring former felons. In addition, they are not part of the box ban movement, and there is no indication that they have made a commitment to fair trade. Companies that join the Ban-the-Box initiative do not ask about their felon records before the interview phase. And those who agreed to the Fair Chance Business Pledge make sure there is no discrimination during the hiring process because of a past crime.

After interviewing convicted people who work at Kroger, it is difficult to have a general formula to use here. If the company needs manpower, it will hire.

LYFT

As one of Uber's main competitors, Uber learns from the mistakes of other companies like this. The travel sharing company offers its services on vehicles with different transport capacities, from cars to two-wheelers, including the loan of bicycles.

Founded in the summer of 2012, it is one of the companies that has grown exponentially over the past seven years. With approximately 5,000 employees handling backend and driving profiles, the company is one that is growing exponentially due to the increasing number of people who have started using taxis.

While there is no conclusive evidence that can be provided in this book, such as the testimony of a former felon who now works at Lyft, various Internet sources suggest that Lyft (and Uber both) hire former workers. felons. They do not have a specialized program for felons as such and do not support the Ban-the-box movement.

The box ban movement is one that involves organizations avoiding asking questions about felon records in writing, online, or offline. This decision, as has already been said, is not part of Lyft, and therefore its employment process may be a little more thorough than usual.

Since they do not support the movement, they are obviously not an organization that has adopted the Fair Chance Business Pledge, which allows ex-offenders to be judged on an equal footing with someone with their own background. and without discrimination in the past.

While these things may seem daunting, you can still make a good impression as long as your CV and your application stand out. So, don't give up hope yet.

LOWE'S

The company loses only to HomeDepot US in the home retail store category. As a chain of stores specializing in home improvement products, the establishment has more than 2,000 branches established in different American states and even in certain parts of Canada. It has more than 300,000 employees and is always looking for more employees to expand to other locations in the United States.

They hire people in five categories, so to speak, and are freight and inventory, management, sales, customer service, and retail. Entry-level jobs are available primarily in the Cargo and Stock, Low-Level Retail and Customer Service categories, with average wages ranging from $ 12 to $ 14 per hour.

Lowe's hires felons. Like most other institutions, there are no special programs for felons, so you are simply recruited as people without crimes. However , we can offer you an entry-level job if your qualifications are not very numerous, but it is much more possible to advance in the management chain if you devote time and effort to developing the skills necessary to move on to managing Lowe.

According to recent updates, it was also discovered that they supported the box ban movement. Ban-the-box is a movement where establishments refrain from asking job seekers for their felon records up to the interview stage.

This gives all individuals a fair chance to get a job when seated for an interview. So to conclude, if Lowe hires felons, they are sure to hire felons and do so without discrimination. Unfortunately, they did not participate in the Fair Chance Business Pledge.

LSG SKY CHEFS

LSG Sky Chefs is the trademark of LSG Lufthansa Service Holding AG, which is the world's largest supplier of food services (although Gate Gourmet claims to be the largest "independent" supplier in the world) and on-board services. It is a branch of Deutsche Lufthansa AG.

Part of the company was owned by AMR Corporation, the parent company of American Airlines. Its main commercial function is to prepare and deliver meals, drinks, and snacks to aircraft for domestic and international flights.

Start your career with the world leader in catering and onboard services. Are you searching for your first job, internship program? They will help you pave the way for professional success.

Are you searching for your first work experience in this jet industry ? Are you still studying? Have you just finished? Whether you are on a sabbatical year or looking for a voluntary internship or compulsory placement as part of your educations, you will gain real industry experience from the first day. They are always looking for enthusiastic and talented people in a wide range of fields of activity.

Are you looking for an interesting company to support you in your practical thesis as part of your course? Join them for a unique opportunity to develop and apply their knowledge to optimize our daily operations. They can't wait to hear your ideas.

MCDONALD'S

McDonald's Corporation is the world's largest hamburger fast-food chain, serving approximately 68 million customers in 119 countries daily at 35,000 locations. A McDonald's restaurant is run by a franchisee, an affiliate, or the business itself.

McDonald's Corporation and McDonald's USA, LLC ("McDonald's") is committed to an equal employment opportunity policy and do not discriminate against any candidate or employee by race, color, sex, religion, age, disability, veteran or military status, sexual orientation, national origin, citizenship status, gender expression / identity, genetic information or any other basis protected legally recognized in accordance with federal, state or local laws, regulations or regulations . Applicants with ill health may be entitled to reasonable accommodation under Americans with Disabilities Act law and certain national and local laws. A sensible accommodation is an adjustment or change to a work or job environment, which guaranteed will be equal opportunities in employment without imposing undue hardship on the operation of the business. Independent franchisees are equal opportunity employers engaged in a diverse and inclusive workforce. Franchisees are independent business people and are not employed by McDonald's. Thus, each franchisee and each franchised restaurant is unique, and the franchisee is solely responsible for all employment matters in his restaurant, including the employment conditions of his employees, such as hiring, firing, discipline, supervision, staff, and schedules. Depending on the location of the restaurant you select, the job you are applying for may be in a restaurant operated and owned by an independent franchisee, not McDonald's. This means that the franchisee, not McDonald's, is responsible for all restaurant employment matters. If you are employed for the job, the franchisee will be your employer, not McDonald's. For franchise restaurants, contact your franchise organization directly as you need help filling out forms or participating in the franchise application process.

METALS USA

Metals USA is a supplier of treated carbon steel, stainless steel, aluminum, red metals, and fabricated metal components. On April 12, 2013, it was acquired by Reliance Steel & Aluminum Company ("Reliance"). Reliance is the largest business center of metal Services of America North and one of the leading suppliers of metal processing services to add value and inventory management.

MOTOROLA

Motorola created the mobile communications industry. He invented most of the protocols and technologies that enable mobile communications, including the first base station, the first cell phone, and almost everything else.

As part of the Lenovo household, Motorola Mobility creates innovative smartphones and accessories designed for the consumer. That is why they are looking for thinkers, innovators, and problem-solvers who believe that we need to work together to contest the status quo. If you share their commitment to creativity and our passion for bringing new possibilities in mobile technology to life, they want you to say hello to Moto.

Motorola has a long history of inventing revolutionary technology. As a member of the Motorola team, you will help them continue their legacy by collaborating with gifted colleagues from around the world to create new products that are not only different but better. They thrive in an open and united culture, working in teams where their contribution has an impact. They believe in transparency at all levels of the company, value everyone's opinion, and encourage new ways of thinking. Here, everyone takes responsibility for their work, drives consumer-centered decision-making, and enables their staff to advance the line of innovation.

NORDSTORM

Nordstrom, Inc. is an American luxury fashion retailer, founded by John W. Nordstrom and Carl F. Wallin and based in Seattle, Washington. There are 271 stores in 36 states, including 117 full stores and 151 Nordstrom Racks.

Whether you are in sales, inventory, change, or management, or as part of the background glue that holds it all together, we are all obsessed with customer service and, of course, fashion. Exciting and fast, a career at Nordstrom means staying ahead of the trend, going fast, and being part of something we find impressive.

O'CHARLEY

The O'Charley is a chain of casual restaurants in the United States, with over 200 owned by local society. O'Charley's is located in 17 states in the South and Midwest, including four O'Charley franchise restaurants in Michigan, four O'Charley franchise stores in Ohio, three O'Charley joint ventures restaurants in Louisiana and one O'Charley's joint restaurant in Wisconsin.

O'Charley's Restaurant + Bar is known for offering great food, good times, and some of the most impressive job opportunities on the market.

This is because working at O'Charley's puts you in the company of friends and professionals who really enjoy working together. In fact, O'Charley's is recognized as best in a class by People Report magazine and Chain Leader for our team member sponsorship program.

PACTIV

Pactiv is one of the world ' s largest manufacturers and distributors of food packaging and foodservice, providing slaughterhouses, processors, supermarkets, restaurants, institutions and foodservice establishments in America North.

Pactiv LLC is a company that offers equal opportunities. They consider candidates for all positions regardless of race, color , religion, national origin, gender, ancestry, citizenship, sexual orientation, gender identity , marital status, age, disability, protected veteran status or any other legally protected status.

PAPPADEAUX

Pappas Restaurants is a group of private restaurants based in Houston, Texas. The founders are the Greek American brothers Pete and Jim Pappas. The Pappas family has launched 8 unique restaurants with over 80 locations in Texas, Colorado, Arizona, Illinois, Ohio,

New Mexico, and Georgia. In the December 2007 issue of Texas per Month, Pappas Bros. Steakhouse has been voted the best steakhouse in Texas.

They are an employer guaranteeing equal opportunities M / F / D / V / A. They devote themselves to a policy of employment practices which prohibits discrimination against any candidate or employee with regard to "race, national origin, gender, color , citizenship status, age, religion, mental or physical disability , veteran status, genetic information, and all factors protected by law. "

PETSMART

PetSmart, Inc. is a retail chain that operates in the United States, Canada, and Puerto Rico that sells specialized pet supplies and services such as dog care and training, boarding facilities for cats and dogs, and nursery school. PetSmart also offers a diverse selection of animals for sale and adoption, such as birds, fish, amphibians, reptiles, and various breeds of small animals such as guinea pigs, chinchillas, gerbils, hamsters, and mouses.

There is one thing that unites everyone who works at PetSmart: everyone loves animals. Cats, dogs, goldfish, parakeets, hamsters - you choose, they love them. Every day, they combine their passion for creating something incredible: a place for our many best friends to be healthy, happy, and keep the line moving!

When you work with them, you find that they also love your people. Whether in a shop, a center of the distribution , or in our home office, you will feel inspired and empowered to go beyond, to go further, and make the most of your career with PetSmart.

PEPSICO

PepsiCo Inc. is a multinational American food and beverage company based in Purchase, United States, New York, with interests in the marketing, manufacturing, and distribution of snack foods, beverages, and other grain products.

At PepsiCo, you achieve the best of both worlds: the mindset, the reach, and the resources of an entrepreneur. Its collaborative culture and global presence generate a flow of new opportunities to shape the future and drive the work of your life. Bring your unique perspective. Bring curiosity. Bring creativity and dynamism. They offer you a platform to dare on a global scale.

PHILLIP MORRIS

Philip Morris International Inc. is a global cigarette and tobacco company in the United States, with products sold in over 200 nations, with 15.6% of the international cigarette market outside the United States. The company's most recognized and best-selling product is Marlboro.

At PMI, you will work in regions, cultures, roles, and disciplines. You will be chanced to learn from experts in your field. As part of a global team, you will blend into a wide variety of nationalities and backgrounds. You will be allowed to take responsibility and expand your team beyond the sum of its parts. If PMI looks like your type of business, contact us.

Take the initiative to make an impact. Constantly experiment, learn, and take risks. Have a vision and bring it to life by challenging the status quo. Have the courage to defend new ideas with conviction. Do you believe you have what it takes to work with them? In this case, we would be delighted to speak to you.

PILGRIM'S

For over six decades, Pilgrim produces healthy food and high quality, which are ã the one found in some - some of the best recipes in the world. It is dedicated to the provision of these healthy products will LEVELS and high quality for O optimum, enabling everyone to eat well.

As the leading provider of recruiting technology, we know how important it is to hire the right people. But hiring is only half the story. At iCIMS, they believe in extending the same first-class experience they offer to our clients and candidates to their employees. And they take the time to do it - in fact, they ranked as one of NJBIZ's best workplaces in New Jersey for the eighth consecutive year and reached 16th place on the 2019 Glassdoor Best Workplaces List .

Collectively, they have cultivated a unique corporate culture in which employees respect, support, celebrate, and learn from each other while having a real and measurable impact: on our customers, our businesses, and others. If you want to work with other hardworking, bright, and fun people, you will feel at home.

PRAXAIR

Praxair, Inc. is an industrial gas company. It is the largest industrial gas company in North and South America and the third in the world in terms of turnover.

At Praxair, you will bring together talented and diverse people who work to make a difference in the world and make the business prosper. Its employees work on stimulating and meaningful projects and are confident of assuming their responsibilities early in their careers. Your contributions are invaluable to the company, customers, communities, and shareholders. Explore the site and find out how your talent can impact Praxair.

RADISSON

Radisson Hotels is a multinational hotel company with over 420 locations in 73 nations. The first Radisson Hotel was constructed in 1909 in Minneapolis, Minnesota, USA. It owes its name to the 17th-century French explorer , Pierre-Esprit Radisson. Curt Carlson (1914 - 1999) purchased the hotel in 1962 and still belongs to Carlson.

Join them in their mission to make every moment matter now for their guests, business partners, and themselves. Explore here the great opportunities for you to serve, expand, grow... and be part of the most inspired hotel industry in the world.

At the Radisson Hotel Group, they believe that people are their first asset. As one of the greatest hotel companies in the globe, it is always looking for great people to join its team. If it sounds like an ambition you share, start with them.

RED LOBSTER

Red Lobster is an American casual restaurant chain based in Orlando, Florida. The company is present in Canada, Saudi Arabia, the United Arab Emirates, Qatar, and Japan, as well as in the United States. As of 23rd of February, 2013, there were 705 red lobster locations worldwide.

RED ROBBIN

Red Robin Gourmet Burgers or simply Red Robin is a chain of casual restaurants founded in 1969 in Seattle, Washington, and now headquartered in Greenwood Village, Colorado.

Red Robin is an employer ensuring equality of opportunity and electronic verification, committed to a diverse workforce. Independent Red Robin franchisees hire their own employees and set their own terms and conditions, which may differ from those described.

RESTAURANT DEPOT

Restaurant Depot, a division of Jetro Holdings, LLC based in College Point, New York, has provided quality food products and shipping warehouse stores to independent food companies since 1990. Eliminating the overhead of a distributor Traditionally focused on the needs of independent foodservice providers and offering free membership, Restaurant Depot has become the primary low-cost alternative to other food service providers in the United States.

REYES BEVERAGE GROUP

Re yes Holdings, LLC is an American foodservice wholesaler and distributor. Its divisions include McDonald's distributor Martin-Brower, food service company Reinhart FoodService, and beer distributor Reyes Beverage Group. In 2010, it was the 20th biggest private organization in the United States. The organization is based in Rosemont, Illinois, a suburb of Chicago.

RUBBERMAID

Rubbermaid is an American distributor and manufacturer of many household items. It is a subsidiary of Newell Rubbermaid. It is best known for the production of food storage containers and garbage cans. It also produces sheds, benches, cupboards and shelves, clothing baskets, and other household items.

RUBY TUESDAY

Ruby Tuesday Inc. is an American international foodservice retailer that owns, franchises, and operates Ruby Tuesday restaurants. They are headquartered in Maryville, Tennessee, and operate 755 sites worldwide, among their different concepts. As of 2nd of June, 2015, Ruby Tuesday, Inc. had Ruby Tuesday restaurants owned and / or franchised in 44 states and 13 foreign countries. The company-owned and operated 658 Ruby Tuesday restaurants, while national and international franchisees operated 29 and 49 restaurants, respectively. Its international locations include Canada, Chile, Greece, Egypt, El Salvador, Guam, Honduras, Hong Kong, Iceland, India, Kuwait, Romania, Saudi Arabia, Trinidad, United Arab Emirates, Panama, and the United Kingdom.

RUMPKE

Rumpke Waste & Recycling has been dedicated to keeping business and neighborhoods clean and green since 1932 by providing green waste disposal solutions and recycling options. Based in Colerain Township, Ohio.

SAFEWAY

Safeway is an American supermarket chain acquired in early 2014 by Cerberus Capital Management. The merged company has more than 2,400 stores, of which 1,335 operates under Safeway flags and more than 250,000 employees, making it the second-largest supermarket chain in North America.

SALVATION ARMY

The Salvation Army is a denominational Christian church and a structured quasi-military international charity. The organization has more than 1.5 million members worldwide, made up of soldiers, officers, and supporters known as Salvationists.

The Salvation Army, a multinational movement, is an evangelical part of the Universal Christian Church. Your message is based on the Bible. Your ministry is driven by the love of God. Its mission is to preach the gospel of

Jesus Christ and respond to human needs on his behalf without discrimination.

The Salvation Army is an employer guaranteeing equal opportunities and is committed to providing all applicants and employees with a respectful environment, free from discrimination or unlawful harassment based on age, race, color, religion, gender, national origin, and marital status. , disability, citizenship, sexual orientation, gender identity, gender expression, or any other characteristic protected by law. This equal employment opportunity will apply to recruitment and hiring, training, promotion, wages, and other remuneration, transfers, and layoffs or layoffs.

SARA LEE

Sara Lee Corporation was an American consumer goods company based in Downers Grove, Illinois. It is present in more than 40 countries and has sold its products in more than 180 countries around the world. Its international operations were based in Utrecht, the Netherlands.

SEARS

Sears (officially Sears, Roebuck & Company) is an American chain of department stores. The organization was created by Alvah Curtis Roebuck and Richard Warren Sears in 1886. It is the fourth largest US wholesale business since October 2013 (behind Walmart, Target, Best Buy, and Home Depot), and it is the twelfth country's largest retailer in general.

SEASONS 52

Seasons 52 is an internal fine-dining chain owned and developed in the United States by Darden Restaurants, Inc. in 2003. The brand's concept is to offer a sophisticated atmosphere, a seasonal menu, and fresh ingredients to offer an option low calorie compared to your competitors.

Seasons 52 is always looking for enthusiastic and hardworking people dedicated to exceptional service and the culinary arts.

SHELL OIL

Shell Oil Company is the American subsidiary of Royal Dutch Shell, a large Anglo-Dutch oil multinational, which is among the largest oil companies in the world. In the United States, approximately 22,000 Shell employees are based. The US headquarters are located in Houston, Texas.

SHOPRITE

ShopRite Supermarkets is a retail's cooperative chain of supermarkets in the northeast of the United States, with stores in Pennsylvania, New York, New Jersey, Connecticut, Delaware, and Maryland. Based in Keasbey, New Jersey, ShopRite is made up of 50 individually owned and operated subsidiaries with more than 296 stores, all under its corporate and distribution arm, Wakefern Food Corporation.

SONY

Sony Corporation is the electronics organization unit and parent company of the Sony group, which operates in its four business segments - electronics (including video games, network services and medical), film, music, and financial services.

Each of us has an imagination - this unique ability to visualize. To create. Innovate. But when was the last time you put it to work? If you want to do more, you've come to the right place and in the right business.

Sony Electronics is an employer providing equal access to employment and affirmative action and provides reasonable accommodation to qualified people with disabilities and disabled veterans in the application process.

STARBUCKS

Starbucks is a chain of retail cafes in the United States with a global presence. It was founded in Seattle in 1971. It specializes in a variety of coffee drinks, unique to the flavor and brand of the company. Starbucks operates in over 30,000 locations worldwide and has a huge employee list of over 291,000 employees. The company is driving the craze for artisanally roasted coffee. In turn, the demand for this coffee has increased exponentially in recent years. In 2018, the company generated revenue of $ 24.71 billion.

Starbucks is hiring felons. The company does not take into account your background but expects you to be sincere and open in your application. If you are on the final list, the company will do a felon background check on a case by case basis. This helps Starbucks prioritize candidates based on their relevance to the position in question. They then find and choose what best suits their needs. If you have a misdemeanor or a crime on your part, Starbucks will provide you with an equal playing field, which will ensure that there is no discrimination or prejudice against you during the hiring process.

Starbucks has made a commercial commitment to "ban the box" and be part of the campaign. This means that they do not ask personal questions about their background in the application form or the interview process. Only if you are selected will you be asked a few questions, and a background check will be done to determine your candidacy for the position in question.

Remember that society has no specific plans to recover felons and convicted offenders. Although this does not mean that you face discrimination in the workplace, it just means that you will not have dedicated facilities and services available in companies that have specific programs for felons.

SUBWAY

Subway is an American fast-food franchise that mainly sells sandwiches and undersea salads. It is owned and operated by Doctor's Associates, Inc. Subway is one of the fastest-growing franchises in the world, with 43,035 restaurants in 108 countries and territories on November 15, 2014.

SYSCO

Sysco is an American multinational company specializing in the marketing and distribution of food products to restaurants, facilities and medical education, hotels, and other foodservice and hospitality businesses. The organization is based in the Energy Corridor of Houston, Texas.

At Sysco, they offer a set of benefits that meet the unique needs of their diverse team of members, from a medical plan with a variety of options to choose from, to a 401 (k) plan that allows your employees to work and plan. the retirement they dream of. But that's not all! They are proud of their benefits and encourage you to discover how Sysco provides good benefits to its members and their families at all stages of life.

TARGET

Target Corporation was founded by George Dayton in 1902 and based in Minneapolis. The company is the 8th largest US retailer with revenues of $ 75.356 billion (EF 2019). This chain of stores offers a wide variety of product segments, from beauty and health to toys and games. Target currently operates more than 1,800 stores nationwide and employs approximately 360,000 people in its departments.

As you already know, Target does not hesitate to give felons a chance. Target also commits crimes. However, it depends on different cases. It usually depends on the duration of your crime and what it was. According to some sources, they certainly do not accept former felons for crimes such as assault, sex crimes, and assault, while DUI and drug-related crimes can still be accepted.

Target believes in diversity, inclusion, and ensures that everyone has the same platform to move forward in life. She believes in recruiting sincere, dedicated, and talented staff in doing the necessary work, regardless of their past felon history. Target strives to understand the impact of a person's felony record on their ability to seek employment.

TELEPERFORMANCE

Teleperformance is a global company, a world leader in multi-channel customer experience. Created in 1978 by Daniel Julien, the company specializes in customer service, technical support, the center calls , debt collection, and social media. The company operates approximately 135,000 computer workstations, with more than 175,000 employees in 270 contact centers in 62 countries.

TESLA

Tesla Motors, Inc. is an American organization that designs, produces, and sells electric cars and powertrain components for electric vehicles. Tesla attracted attention following the production of Tesla Roadster, the first fully electric sports car.

At Tesla, they solve the most important problems in the world with talented people who share their passion for changing the world. Their culture is fast, energetic, and innovative. Based in the San Francisco Bay Zone, with offices around the world, they work to create an inclusive setting in which all individuals, regardless of age, gender, race, religion, or background, can the best job possible.

TOY 'R' US

Toys "R" Us, Inc. (stylized as Toys? Us) is an American toy and youth product retailer founded in 1948 and headquartered in Wayne, New Jersey. The company operates more than 893 Babies "R" Us and Toys "R" Us stores in the US, more than 730 international stores and more than 205 licensed stores in 36 countries and jurisdictions.

TRADING JOES

Trader Joe's is a private American chain of specialty supermarkets based in Monrovia, California, in Greater Los Angeles. As of May 16, 2014, Trader Joe's had a total of 418 stores. About half of its stores are in California, with the greatest concentration in southern California, but the organization also has locations in 38 other states and in Washington, DC.

At Trader Joe's, they create an exceptional customer experience around the discovery and tasting of incredible dishes and drinks. This is what they do, and their team is the bread and butter, to the side of the bread and butter of Trader Joe's.

They are looking for fun, hardworking people - people who are passionate about eating, learning, and enjoying others. They take the work seriously, dress -If lightly and always try to improve your team.

TYSON FOOD

Tyson Foods, Inc. is an American multinational based in Springdale, Arkansas, which operates in the food industry. The company is the second-largest processor and marketer of chicken, beef, and pork in the world, just behind the Brazilian JBS SA, and exports the largest percentage of beef from the United States each year.

At Tyson, they embrace the diversity of their team members, customers, stakeholders, and consumers - their unique backgrounds, experiences, thoughts, and talents. All are appreciated and appreciated for their distinctive contributions.

U-HAUL

U-Haul is a moving equipment storage and equipment rental company based in Phoenix, Arizona, operating since 1945. The company was founded by Leonard Shoen (LS "Sam" Shoen) in Ridgefield, Washington, who started his garage activity belonging to his wife's family and expanded by franchises with petrol stations.

UPS

UPS is a multinational company based in the United States and a leader in supply chain management and package delivery. Over the years, UPS have spread their wings and have ventured into other areas, such as air travel, in partnership with All Nippon Airways. However, the main thing was and remains package delivery. With a few acquisitions and associations, they have established their global presence in this area.

UPS is a global package delivery and supply chain management company. Therefore, it has great potential for employing people. But then, do they hire former felons? Yes, they do. However, they will consider it on a case-by-case basis, but not all.

UPS is a customer-centric business, and its primary concern is always to satisfy its customers. Consequently, all the packages that the company processes go through a rigorous procedure. This process only ends when this package is safely delivered to the person or business to which it is addressed. It takes a lot of commitment and dedication to complete this process. And this is accomplished by UPS with its highly committed and professional service. In other words, your positions must be occupied by highly motivated and dedicated people who share the mission of the company. Therefore, the people they are looking for must have these qualities and be trustworthy.

The organization does not have a written policy on the employment of felons. However, the official hiring declaration indicates that they are an employer guaranteeing equal opportunities. The company does not discriminate and makes all of its employment decisions in accordance with applicable laws. Some sources have revealed that they are hired on a case-by-case basis and that for some time, they have hired ex-offenders in specific positions.

US FOOD

US Foods (formerly US Foodservice) is one of the leading distributors in the United States. With almost $ 19 billion in annual revenue, US Foods is the 10th largest private company in America. The company hires approximately 25,000 people at more than 60 locations across the country and supplies food and related products to over 250,000 customers, including independent multi-unit restaurants, healthcare and hospitality facilities, institutions governmental and educational.

US STEEL CORPORATION

United States Steel Corporation, better known as US Steel, is an integrated steel producer in the United States with significant production activities in the United States, Canada, and Central Europe. The company was the 13th largest steel producer in the world in 2010.

They look forward to the opportunity to welcome you to your business.

They are dedicated to attracting and retaining a diverse group of talented employees - people whose different skills, ideas, backgrounds, and talents continually lead to innovative approaches to business solutions, technological advancements, and our collective strength.

United States Steel Corporation, its subsidiaries, and certain affiliates ("US Steel") are employers with equal opportunities. It is your policy to offer equal employment opportunities (EEO) based on professional qualifications, without discrimination based on race, color, age, religion, ancestry, national origin, genetics, sexual orientation, sex, gender identity, employment status. disability or protected veteran status or another legally protected group status.

VOLUNTEERS OF AMERICA

Volunteers of America is an organization non-profit founded on the faith that provides services affordable supportive housing and other mainly low - the people returned to the United States. Based in Alexandria, Virginia, the organization includes 36 affiliates who serve approximately 400 communities in 46 states, Puerto Rico and District of Columbia.

At Volunteers of America, they are more than a non-profit organization. It is a service ministry that includes nearly 16,000 employees and more than 55,000 volunteers with a common vision of a world where all people live in security with social, physical and emotional well-being, spiritual fulfillment, justice, and hope.

The national office is situated in Alexandria, Virginia, part of the greater Washington, DC area. Headquarters includes key management and office staff who have national responsibilities and support local offices and homes for Volunteer America and the living and care communities: communications, fundraising, public policy, finance, charter, housing, program services, volunteer services, and other operations.

WALGREENS

Walgreens is a US drugstore retail chain that is available nationwide. The company was founded in Chicago, Illinois, over 100 years ago. They have approximately 9,277 stores in 50 states. This makes it the second-largest chain of pharmacies in the United States. In addition to purchasing prescription drugs, Walgreens also specializes in dispensing prescriptions, health products, photographic services, and more. In 2014, the company acquired 50% of Alliance Boots and created Walgreens Boots Alliance. Walgreens became one of the subsidiaries of this newly created company. Its headquarters are in Deerfield, Illinois.

To put it bluntly, Walgreens has no specific policy on whether or not to hire former felons. But there is no reason to worry. Many organizations have changed their internal policies to accommodate former felons. While not visible on the surface, it is known that Walgreens has hired former felons in the past without any discrimination, which seems like a good indication to you. The simple process of hiring the company does not discriminate against its candidates. This ensures that you have a fair chance at the position in question.

WALMART

With more than 2.4 million employees, Walmart is a renowned chain of hypermarkets and grocery stores. They operate in 27 countries. They have several job profiles ranging from delicatessen support to data scientists. The company is the amalgam of the efforts of each employee.

Some of the entry-level jobs in the business include employees, operators, delivery people, etc. Most of the time, payment for these entry-level jobs are made hourly. The average salary in different fields ranges from $ 10 to

$ 15. The very existence of this book is to ensure that Walmart hires felons.

Some questions you may have to include the possibility that Walmart will refuse you if you have committed a crime. In this case, there is certainly nothing to worry about, since Walmart tenants go through these things. However, you will have to convince them that you have changed since you committed the crime.

WENDY'S

Wendy's is an international fast-food chain founded by Dave Thomas on November 15, 1969, in Columbus, Ohio, United States. The company moved its headquarters in Dublin, Ohio, on January 29, 2006. Approximately 77% of Wendy's restaurants are franchised; the majority is in America 's north. Wendy's and its subsidiaries employ more than 47,000 people in their global operations.

WINCO FOOD

WinCo Foods, Inc. is a private American supermarket chain in Boise, Idaho, with retail stores in Arizona, California, Idaho, Nevada, Oregon, Utah, Washington, and Texas. As of March 2014, it had 93 retail stores and four distribution centers with 14,200 employees.

As WinCo Foods continues to grow, its diversity - from diverse perspectives and a wide range of experiences - is essential to its strategy and success. They are committed to continuing to cultivate and celebrate an inclusive environment in which all employees are respected and valued of race, color , religion, gender, sexual orientation, identity: gender, national origin, veteran status, or disability status.

XEROX

Xerox Corporation Ltd is an American multinational document management company that produces and sells a variety of color printers and black and white multifunction systems, copiers, digital production printers , and related consulting services and supplies.

They help businesses and governments improve the workflow to improve performance, agility, and transformation. They stay true to their heritage, solving business problems with diverse services, innovative technologies, and the expertise of Xerox employees.

YARD HOUSE

When the craft beer revolution started almost 20 years ago, Yard House was there, leading the way. Taking its vast brewing and brewing experience and pairing it with a kitchen that prepares over 100 daily items from scratch, Yard House has become a modern public place where food and beer lovers get together.